THE INFINITY CURE

T.A. Berkeley

ALSO BY T.A. BERKELEY

Eternal Order

The galaxy's biggest reality star is murdered on the grounds of a secretive religious order. To investigate, rookie police detective Lyndon Bates must leave his body behind and venture onto planet Halcyon as a woman. But the murder is only one of the mysteries lurking within the walls of the deceptively idyllic convent.

Devil's Sanctum

A perfect date becomes a nightmare when a man's new love disappears. And it seems there was a lot he didn't know about his girlfriend. To find her, he embarks on a twisted adventure where his only friend is someone he isn't sure he can trust.

Viral

In this paranormal polyamorous horror thriller, eight teens go to rural West Virginia for what they think will be a carefree vacation. But it turns nightmarish when one starts to read the others' thoughts—including a dark secret about the real reason they left town. Now the group must grapple with a terrifying virus they've brought with them.

READER PRAISE FOR *VIRAL*

"Swift and captivating, T.A. Berkeley's debut novel grabs you from the beginning and doesn't let go as it pulls you along for an eerie and exciting ride!"

"Delicious horror-mystery with plenty of paranoia and psychological mayhem to breeze right through without putting it down."

"Such a fun summer read! … The writing is lean and moves quickly."

"A great, fun thriller (with some saucy bits in there too) that kept me guessing to the end!"

For B.A. and T.N., the reasons I'm able to do what I
love

CHAPTER ONE

The sun glared harshly from a cloudless sky as Hiroe stepped from the cool air of the cab onto the scorching pavement.

Eager to escape it, she hurried along a concrete path toward the water, the empty beach on either side of her fenced off from the public and lined with hybrid palm cactus — short spiny trunks supporting spreading leaves, the tops adorned with bright blooms. In the distance, dozens of sunbathers crowded under large ultraviolet and heat protection screens that stretched across the sand.

By the time she neared the water, gray clouds had begun to collect on the horizon. The air cooled and the waves became rougher as the rolling, darkening masses rapidly approached. The beach's occupants, a handful at first, then all of them, began to gather their belongings and hurry toward bars and cars for shelter.

Hiroe quickened her stride, glancing repeatedly at the gathering storm. Ordinarily she would've found it hard to approach a large body of water, but the storm looked like it was going to be a bad one. She tried to ignore the ocean and focus on her destination: a small square building that started on the beach and extended into the shallows.

Crackles of lightning sliced hectically through the charcoal depths of the clouds. Her fingers lightly held the strap on a suitcase that moved faster to match her pace. As she approached, the door slid open and a man inside beckoned her.

The wind was picking up and fat drops of rain had begun hitting the ground around her.

The temperature had dropped but the air was still hot, only now it contained a suffocating humidity. Lapping water from the rising tide sucked at her feet as if to pull her in. Shuddering, she jogged the last few steps, feet squelching against her wet sandals, and stepped into the structure with relief.

The door moved silently closed behind her, cutting off the sound of the approaching storm. "Just in time," she said to the man, his features coming into focus as her eyes adjusted to the dimness. They stood together in a small space devoid of doors or furniture, though art adorned the walls.

He nodded, lips thinning into a small tight smile. He was dressed in a slate gray suit that matched the steely color of his precisely close-cropped hair. He blinked several times rapidly and his eyes scanned her. "Ms. Anno," he said when he'd retrieved her identification.

"That's me," Hiroe said. "Am I the last one?"

He didn't seem to hear her question. "Right this way." He turned and the solid-looking wall behind him split in two, revealing another room. Hiroe followed him inside, where a chaise lounge with plump cushions awaited. Lifting a pitcher from a shelf, the man poured a small amount of clear liquid into a tumbler, which he held out to her. "This will help your body with the pressure changes," he told her. "Are you prone to claustrophobia or anxiety?" With his other hand he held up a tiny vial of greenish-blue gel.

Hiroe accepted the glass but shook her head at the other offer. "No more than usual," she said, her voice betraying her with a slight tremor.

If he noticed, the man didn't question it. He tapped a circular patch on the wall next to the chaise and soft, slow flute music began to play. "You can change it if you like," he told her. "Be sure to finish your drink, please. This door will open when it's time to go." He pointed at the wall opposite the one they'd come through, which also gave no indication of having a doorway in it. Then he left the way he'd come in. The door closed and again appeared to be a solid seamless wall.

Hiroe perched on the edge of the chaise. The cushion sank comfortingly, but her posture remained stiff. It was an odd feeling, being in a room with no visible openings, and knowing it was partly underwater increased the feeling of being trapped. She took a couple deep gulps of air, filling her lungs to reassure them there was plenty of oxygen. Tapping the circle on the wall restlessly, she cycled through various somnolent songs and noises.

A channel of ocean sounds popped up. Hiroe switched quickly to one with classical acoustic guitar music and left it there. She remembered the drink and downed half of it in a gulp, barely tasting the liquid, which was subtly sweet with a hint of citrus and carbonation. She stood and paced the small room, drinking the remainder in small frequent sips as she looked inattentively at the blandly pleasant art adorning the walls.

The other door slid open without warning, and she set her empty glass down, taking up the leash attached to her suitcase. It followed her down a short hallway to a capsule-like vessel that stood open, hovering several inches above the floor.

She entered gingerly, waiting for it to wobble when she stepped onto it, but the craft stayed stable. The door closed as soon as her suitcase cleared it. Hiroe settled into a seat that automatically strapped her in. There were no visible controls. A light hum arose, barely audible, and the vessel began to move smoothly forward and down into a sloping tunnel.

It touched on the surface of gently lapping water and skimmed along for a second before dipping lower. Hiroe's breath caught in her throat as the water line rose on the windshield. For a few moments, as the capsule submerged completely and continued to sink, it became dark outside the vessel and she saw nothing but her reflected image in front of her, her mouth downturned, her face ashen under her bangs. She ran her fingers through her salt-and-pepper (still mostly pepper at this point) hair, instinctively fluffing and smoothing her pageboy cut as she attempted to rearrange her features into a more stoic expression.

Then her vehicle burst out of the tunnel into the ocean—the motion was seamless but the sudden appearance of light nearly made her jump. Now she was gliding through blue-green water lit from some unknown source—surely they were too far down for it to be the sun, and even if they weren't, the storm on the surface was probably raging at full force by now.

As the expanse of water opened around her, Hiroe was temporarily distracted from her anxiety. Her vessel floated past reefs of brightly colored coral. Fish and other marine life of impossibly varied shapes and colors flitted through the clear water on either side.

She had no names for the species she saw. A creature with an eel-like shape and iridescent scales snaked its way past her windshield. An orange sphere with pulsing blue organs showing through its skin rotated slowly, buoyed by the currents her capsule created. A school of small, triangular zebra-striped fish with oversize eyes on either side of their heads seemed to stare at her as they undulated in formation, turning as a single body this way and that. Hiroe had never seen so much sea life in one place—not for over forty years, anyway.

Not that she'd sought it out. In fact she'd strenuously objected to this particular assignment. Incredulity had been her initial reaction. "You know I won't do that," she told her editor with a hint of irritation. "Find someone else."

He'd sighed and avoided her eyes at first. "We want our best reporter on it, and that's you," he said. "But, and I hate to have to say this, you're not exactly in a position to pick and choose assignments. It's been decided. You're the best I have, but Hiroe, you're still expendable. There are hundreds, *thousands* of younger people who would kill for a secure position and a decent salary."

Answered by stony silence, he'd continued. "This isn't any ordinary little society function. It's practically a U.N. summit, yet it was announced and apparently organized in the space of a couple weeks. We need someone who's going to be able to get the whole story." He'd sighed. "I'll go to my second best if I have to, but if you turn down this assignment, he's going to become my top reporter after that, because you'll be gone and there'll be nothing I can do to help you."

The words still stung as Hiroe remembered them. She supposed she'd suspected she was losing clout in the organization as she got older, but no one had ever said it to her in quite that way before. She'd never felt forced to do an assignment.

Of course, she'd never been very picky—in fact, sometimes less-interesting assignments intrigued her more because finding the story in it would be a challenge. So she had no idea if she'd have gotten this kind of pushback had she tried to refuse a job in the past. All she knew was she didn't want to chance finding a position at another organization and in the current job market at her age.

Even knowing all this, she'd found a dozen reasons to delay her departure, drawing out her preparations and turning back for forgotten items, and now she was in danger of missing the opening ceremonies altogether. But she was on her way at last.

Hiroe's craft moved fast and the ocean teemed with activity around her, but inside it was calm and stable-feeling, with no physical sensation of motion. The dissonance was unsettling and her stomach flipped as her body struggled to reconcile what she felt with what her eyes were taking in. She took slow shallow breaths until her nausea gradually dissipated.

Just as she was becoming acclimated to the experience, the vessel shot out over a sudden drop-off and began to descend again. Hiroe gasped at the vista that appeared.

CHAPTER TWO

A compound of buildings came into view below her, connected by tunnel-like structures. Her craft approached the largest, an ornate mansion shimmering through the water.

It looked as though it had been plucked from one of the nearby historic Colonial America sites on land and dropped onto the floor of the ocean, though much larger than the homes of the founding fathers she'd visited on school trips as a child.

The compound was surrounded by an aquatic version of stately gardens that stretched farther than Hiroe could see. Groves of seaweed waved with the currents. Coral grew in the shape of statues and abstract sculpture. A netted area contained dozens of translucent purple jellyfish. The estate seemed endless. And it was all lit in the same unidentifiable way as the first stretch of open ocean she'd entered.

Her capsule slid up to and inside a transparent bubble attached to the front of the building. With a rush, the water emptied from the bubble; leftover droplets were chased from the surface by air jets and sucked through grates. When the interior of the bubble was nearly dry, the vessel opened and Hiroe stepped out.

On cue, the massive and intricately decorated front door—which appeared to be made of a carved wood, something like mahogany, though she knew it couldn't be—swung inward. Hiroe was ushered in by an attendant who could've been a twin of the man who had greeted her on the surface.

She stood in an expansive foyer. Unlike the historical appearance of the home's exterior, in here were gleaming modern surfaces and abstract art. As she turned in a circle, taking it all in, Hiroe noticed large windows—entire sections of the wall, in fact—displaying the colorful ocean life surrounding the home.

She knew there hadn't appeared to be windows of this size from the outside. The building's exterior had looked like solid brick.

The attendant had patiently waited for her to finish looking around. Now he took her suitcase and led her to another ornate door. "The guests are gathering in here before the program begins," he told her. "Please feel free to join them; I'll have your luggage taken to your room in the guest suite. First though, madam, I apologize for the intrusion, but I'm required to make sure you don't have any recording devices on you."

He blinked rapidly and looked her up and down. "Thank you," he said after several seconds. "Your hostess understands the unusual nature of this request and thanks you for your cooperation."

Hiroe shrugged off his thanks, but he was right. It was an almost unprecedented request, in fact, and had caused quite a stir at her organization. Her colleagues were simultaneously outraged and fascinated.

The thought of not having any recordings—visual, audio, or otherwise—of the event was nearly inconceivable. Not being able to broadcast it in real time—having to wait until the reporters returned to the surface—made the whole affair seem like a historical oddity. But the consensus was that the delay due to secrecy might actually end up making the story more intriguing to audiences.

Hiroe's editor had told her they'd probably end up doing virtual recreations through computer animation for the entire story—but that made her ability to capture and retain the details of the event even more crucial. The other news agencies would likely do something similar, so it was important to her service that she be as accurate and reliable a source as possible. If their accounts varied, Global Media had to be confident in hers.

Before she left, she had to have her in-body camera, microphone, navigator and phone all surgically removed. It was a painless procedure that took mere minutes—no different than when she went in for repairs or upgrades—but without the technology she'd lived with for years, she felt at first like she'd had part of her brain cut out, so basic were they to her everyday existence.

She hadn't even realized how much she leaned on them to get her through tasks until she had to function without them for a day or two. Her vision seemed less vivid, her memory less sharp when she could no longer instant-replay anything that interested her or when she wanted to recall an exact conversation or incident.

She'd obtained an antique watch so she could at least be aware of time now that her internal clock had been taken away from her. She found herself checking it frequently, each time with a feeling of disappointment that it only had that one piece of information to impart to her.

With a little digging she'd managed to find a foldable tablet, a piece of long-obsolete technology that would help her at least take notes, but her tech team had to remove the camera, take out the microphone and other recording apps and sensors, and wipe it of all connectivity functions. It wouldn't be able to transcribe her thoughts or observations; she couldn't even dictate into it. Now it would only let her type, or write or draw with her finger or a stylus.

She put her hand in her pocket to make sure the device was there, and glanced at her watch to make sure it seemed to be working. Then she squared her shoulders and smiled at the attendant.

The man opened the door; it looked heavy but swung open smoothly with barely a touch from him, in a way that suggested machinery was built into it, and that it too was made of some other material than what it appeared to be.

The cavernous room rang with conversation and laughter. Hiroe hadn't been sure if she'd have an opportunity to change and was glad she'd worn semi-formal clothing on her journey; just black slacks and a navy sequined top, but she wouldn't look too out of place. The other guests were dressed in an array of styles, from gaudy color-shifting illuminated gowns to understated traditional suits and ties.

As she scanned the room, recognizable figures were everywhere. To her left, several scientists she'd learned about in her background research clustered together, deep in heated conversation. They were joined by someone everyone in the room likely knew on sight, Neko Ives. One of the most popular and prolific actors of the past decade, he was also known for his dedication to social causes.

Hiroe watched him passionately gesturing as he spoke to the scientists, seemingly unaware of the stunningly gorgeous woman in a silver minidress who hovered by his side, looking bored at the conversation but possessive of him.

Ives wasn't the only celebrity in the room. Actors, models, athletes, singers, and socialites dotted the room. Some of them stood out immediately; others blended in surprisingly well with the other guests, causing Hiroe to do a double take when she recognized them.

She also saw a few journalists from rival news services; while many people probably wouldn't recognize them right away, they were as familiar to her as any famous actor. Her mouth twisted cynically as she noted how few aqueans there were in the room, given the reason they were all there. The crowd was more than ninety percent human.

Many of the attendees, even though they weren't celebrities Hiroe recognized, seemed accustomed to being in the same room with some of the biggest names in pop culture. Other guests, however, were clearly starstruck, huddling together trying to mask excited whispers and glances across the room at Ives and other famous faces.

Hiroe made her way to the refreshment area, where she gazed admiringly on—then dug shamelessly into—trays of delicate seafood canapes, glistening slices of fresh fruit, light crisp pastries stuffed with dried fruit and sharp cheese, and more. It all tasted real and impossibly fresh, and she saw from the looks on several guests' faces that they may have been experiencing non-laboratory food for the first time in years, or decades. Or ever.

She moved to a bar area where one aquean attendant poured champagne into slender cylindrical glasses and another mixed colorful drinks using unidentifiable ingredients. She accepted a flute of sparkling wine and returned the courteous smile of the girl who handed it to her.

"Can you fucking believe this?" A voice on her left, low but tight with barely suppressed excitement, caused Hiroe to turn. A woman not much younger than her—maybe in her mid-forties—in a tacky ruffled dress gripped a bright pink cocktail and looked hungrily out at the crowd, then back to Hiroe. "That's Mirielle. Like, literally five feet away from us. I cannot.

Believe this is happening!" Her voice rose to a squeak at the end.

"Yeah, amazing," Hiroe agreed politely. She sipped her drink and the two of them stood together, scanning the room. The other woman listed out the names of other celebrity attendees in a reverent whisper, Hiroe nodding and making impressed noises.

When the woman stopped for breath, or ran out of people she recognized, she introduced herself as Lottie Wineman. Her hair looked freshly colored in a rainbow of hues, segments of it painstakingly twisted and fastened to her head in looping patterns. It was obviously an amateur job, but the woman must have spent hours, maybe the entire day, putting it up. It didn't flatter her careworn face, but the amount of effort that had to have gone into it was impressive. "What do you do, Lottie?" Hiroe asked.

"Mostly just on UBI," the woman said distractedly, her eyes ceaselessly roaming from one star to another. "And you know, whatever little tasks I can find to pick up extra money.

Some errand-running gigs, some companionship stuff for lonely old people, that kind of thing. My husband's around here somewhere—oh, he's right over there, man-crushing on Ken Byers."

She gestured toward the tall muscular ballplayer, leaning down to listen to a young woman who was talking animatedly to him, and Hiroe saw a considerably shorter, stockier man in a cheap-looking suit, clutching a tumbler of green liquid and standing a few feet away from the athlete, stealing glances at him. "He hasn't found much work lately so he's been kind of depressed, and following his team's literally the only thing that makes him happy. Or keeps him sane at least."

Lottie smiled at Hiroe, her eyes shining with what could have been tears. "You have no idea how much winning this trip means to us. This is like the best thing that's ever happened to me, ever, by a long shot. And it came at a good time. Shit, we've been talking about splitting up—I mean, we're never gonna make enough money to have kids, so I kinda figure what's the point—but how could we separate? We can barely afford one tiny little apartment together.

"So this just feels like our luck is maybe gonna turn around, you know? This is the most unbelievable thing—I still can't fucking believe I'm looking at all these people in real life. And it's just started, you know? There's all day tomorrow too. It's like—it's like I'm on a vacation with—" she gestured again in another direction "—with Gable Carie. In a fucking underwater mansion that's like a luxury hotel. I mean, what the fuck?"

Hiroe kept nodding as Lottie rambled breathlessly before eventually sputtering to a halt. She'd known several guests would be randomly chosen in a sweepstakes—whether to get more everyday citizens involved in the cause or just to make it seem like a less elitist event, she couldn't say, though she was leaning toward the latter.

Lottery-style contests were more and more common these days; universal basic income kept most people from living in starvation-level poverty (or taking to the streets in protest), but it didn't leave room for anything extra. There wasn't enough work to go around, or free forms of entertainment. Contests and randomly awarded prizes added an element of hope and potential that was missing from many people's lives, and studies had tied them to slowing the growth of the so-called "suicide pandemic." So it wasn't exactly surprising that this event had a lottery aspect. It made for good press.

Lottie spoke again, a welcome interruption from Hiroe's current train of thought. "And you know, where we live, in Montana, we don't really see many, or any, you know—" the woman's voice lowered slightly as she glanced back at the bar "—*aqueans* up close, outside of shows and stuff like that. So that's kind of exciting too. They're so … I don't know, smooth-looking in real life."

She laughed nervously. "I mean, they're great. Great, um, people. This is a really, really … great thing that Faith Benedict is doing for them. Poor things."

Hiroe cringed inwardly at the fumbling, stilted words but politely agreed with the woman. She introduced herself at last, revealing she worked for Global Media, and asked if she could quote Lottie in her reporting about the event.

Lottie's eyes widened and she agreed eagerly. "Maybe not the stuff about Bennie being depressed though, huh? I wouldn't of said that if I'd known it would be in the news!" She giggled some more. "In the news! For real never thought I'd be saying that about myself!"

Aloud, Hiroe agreed readily, but privately she reserved the option to include the detail if it served her story. Unfortunately for Lottie, there wouldn't be much recourse if Hiroe reported something she didn't like. Lawsuits were prohibitively expensive for most people, and viral outrage campaigns were easy to start on social media but always petered out quickly before effecting any real change, the public's attention captured by some new conflict or drama.

Hiroe felt a twinge of pity for the woman. She thought about her returning to her largely directionless life after this weekend and wondered if, in the long run, it would end up making her and her husband's situation feel all the more grim.

CHAPTER THREE

Hiroe got a refill of champagne, said a few parting words to Lottie, and moved away, as if she could escape the depressing vision of her future by putting physical distance between them. The woman barely acknowledged her anyway; she was back to sipping her garishly colored cocktail and drinking in the array of famous guests scattered throughout the crowd.

Hiroe pulled her device from her pocket and quickly typed some of what Lottie had said, along with a few observations about the woman's hair and outfit, her husband, and the couple's excitement about the star-studded crowd.

She roughly sketched the pattern that Lottie's twisted, pinned hair made on her head, the ruffles on her dress, the shape of the cocktail glass she clutched. She was already envisioning the animated recreation of Lottie spouting the quotes. She could feel the familiar irresistible pull toward a good story as it started to take shape in her mind.

Across the vast hall, Hiroe noticed guests milling around a virtual reality chamber with multiple stations. She crossed the room toward it, draining her glass and handing it to an aquean waiter with a tray.

The surfaces of the structure, white with a shimmering pearlescent finish, gave way to holographic images and immersive sounds that came to life around Hiroe as she entered. In the closest station right inside the entrance, she settled onto a seat that looked hard but encased her in customized comfort as soon as it sensed her weight and body shape.

Around her the real world dissolved, replaced by green rippling water. The VR was top quality, realistic to the point of her skin feeling a sensation of cool wetness from the water, although her clothing felt dry. She was submerged in the ocean.

Hiroe's heart jolted unpleasantly and her breath caught in her throat. She closed her eyes, practiced her breathing, and pressed her fingers to her wrist, counting the beats of her pulse until it started to slow to a more normal pace. Then she opened her eyes.

The virtual reality experience had paused when her eyes had shut, but now it resumed. An aquean man swam next to her as she descended into the water, relating the history of human-aquean relations.

The two species had coexisted for eons on the planet, largely unaware of one another. They did encounter one another from time to time, but sightings were brushed off by both sides as legend or hallucinations. Humans developed the myth of mermaids, and some aqueans believed humans were visitors from another planet—if they believed in their existence at all.

Then humans had started deep sea exploration in earnest. The first official contact between the species had sent shockwaves through both their worlds. A joint French and American expedition in the 1970s encountered an aquean village in the Atlantic Ocean and, after exchanging gifts and other friendly gestures, the groups began trying to learn one another's languages. Aquean languages proved impossible for most humans to understand or replicate, but aqueans were able to learn and speak human tongues.

Humans were unable to sustain long visits to the deep ocean, and aqueans couldn't stay healthy for long on land, so even then, relations between them remained limited until technology and medicine advanced enough for humans to exist underwater indefinitely and for aqueans to live on land without suffering adverse side effects.

The virtual reality display went on to focus on the positive influences and contributions aqueans had brought to human society and the ways human technology had aided aqueans, leaving out the most problematic aspects of human-aquean relations.

Some of it was common knowledge, and Hiroe had done background research before she came, so she could fill in the blanks left by the holographic narrator. Because aqueans lived harmoniously with their habitat rather than manipulating it to suit their species, many humans thought of them as primitive and intellectually inferior.

Those perceptions lingered among humans. Aquean societal structures, which eschewed monogamy and contained levels of shared commitments and emotional bonds that transcended the human concepts of blood relations, marriage, and borders, struck many humans as immoral, confusing, or ridiculous.

Relations between the species, while never overtly hostile to the extent of war or invasion, had always been fraught with tensions and conflict. As soon as humans could live underwater, they began trying to purchase land from aqueans. Attempts to impose human concepts of ownership were met with confusion and sometimes outright resistance from aqueans.

And when aqueans became able to survive on land, those who wanted to assimilate into human societies were met with appalling hostility and prejudice by human citizens, media, and political figures alike. It was unsurprising that the VR display avoided such topics, but it also decreased its credibility in Hiroe's mind.

Still, now that she felt calmer, she was enjoying herself. Watching the aquean hologram swim, feeling like she was floating along beside him, gave her a pang of nostalgia. His easy movements reminded her how much she had once loved it herself; the momentum of it, how the water seemed to help her along. After a long day of swimming, being back on land with its gravity and ground and air would feel like something she had to struggle against and through by contrast. She knew he was only a hologram, but the figure beside her radiated that same pleasure and comfort.

The aquean wore only a silvery pair of trunks and she felt hypnotized by his smooth, sea-foam-green skin and the rippling muscles underneath as he took long, unhurried strokes. Curious, she reached out, expecting her hand to go through him as it would with standard quality virtual reality, but instead she felt as if she touched actual skin, smooth and wet, and felt almost embarrassed that she'd touched him. Worse, the hologram responded, glancing at her with a half-smile. She pulled her hand back self-consciously.

The visuals shifted and another ocean vista appeared before them. Hiroe felt more acclimated and her stomach didn't rebel as she was whisked along the seabed through the manicured gardens of Faith Benedict's estate.

Then the plants and fish fell away and she was soaring out over a black fault in the ocean floor, then down into it. Her chest tightened and her breathing became shallow as she fought back panic, trying to listen to the hologram's voice telling her about the spot.

The Infinite Water Trench, as the aquean name for it roughly translated to, was, in their lore, the source of aquean life, the start of their species. Hiroe knew from her research that Faith's decision to build her lavish home close to the trench, essentially making it a feature of her estate, was controversial among many aqueans as well as humans well-versed in their culture. The narration made no mention of that controversy, Hiroe noted wryly even in her nervous state.

Until the emergence of aquamycosis, coming-of-age rites of passage used to be performed at the trench by any aqueans who lived within a month's swim. Every few years, the entire populations of several aquean villages would congregate at Infinite Water.

Aqueans who had turned twenty since the last gathering would travel down together into the trench for a period of fasting and prayer while their communities celebrated above, performing ceremonies to summon health, prosperity, and love for their new adult members.

Participants would forever be considered linked to those they'd dwelt in the trench with, a cohort that, regardless of what village they were from, protected and supported one another for life. It was one of many kinds of community bonds that aqueans considered sacred lifelong commitments.

The exhibit spent a minute or two in total darkness, the whispered prayers in aquean language the only sound Hiroe could hear, the virtual water cold and still around her.

She wrapped her arms around herself, felt her wrist, tried to breathe. Eventually light returned around her as she was brought back out of the trench, and she was in the midst of an aquean ceremony, watching swirling dancers in bright costumes swim in perfect sync as others chanted around them, the distorted sound of their voices traveling through water eerily beautiful.

Hiroe was still relieved when the exhibit ended. She left it wobbling slightly.

CHAPTER FOUR

Hiroe made her way gradually through the room in the other direction, introducing herself to some of the scientists and asking for their thoughts about the gala and aquamycosis.

She jotted notes on her tablet; it captured her scrawls and transcribed them into type, saving them for later. She'd tried the device's touch-screen keyboard but found she was equally slow, if not slower, at typing, having little need to practice either writing or typing in her day-to-day life.

Everything the scientists said on record was predictable and rehearsed. Hiroe was more interested in what she overheard when they weren't talking to her. "Glad to see Faith Benedict only invited real scientists to this thing," one said sarcastically.

His colleague agreed, and they spent a few minutes complaining about her scattershot approach to funding research, which included giving money (and by extension an air of legitimacy) to unethical or ignorant public figures who'd been espousing dangerous theories based on bad science.

Hiroe gathered quotes from lottery winners too, as well as a few of the well-known personalities. She wasn't starstruck but attempted to appear deferential, even when models or athletes tangled their words together and revealed their ignorance of the nature of aquamycosis. She wasn't interested in skewering celebrities. She'd decode and improve their ramblings later during her reporting.

She heard someone shout her name and suppressed annoyance to see two journalists from rival news services waving at her. She pasted on a smile that might have looked genuine enough from across the room, swearing inwardly as they beckoned her.

The three of them chatted politely at first, mainly about the novelty, and constraints, of covering a story without any recording devices.

"Is anyone from Static coming?" asked Perth Roberts, a note of condescension in his voice. A veteran BBC Jazeera reporter, his was the longest-standing and most highly regarded of the four largest worldwide news services. Static was a decade old but still considered an upstart by many in the news business, though it was founded by respected journalists and had attracted many more.

"I wonder if they even got an invitation," said the other journalist, a woman in her twenties, matching his mocking tone. Riva Lorton was relatively new to the scene, but being conventionally pretty and convincingly blond, she had of course quickly risen to prominence in conservative media as a newscaster for Fox RT. Same old story since, what, Katie Couric? Greta something? Hiroe strained to remember the names and faces she'd studied in her broadcast history courses in college, which itself was ancient history — over thirty years ago.

Although she was ambivalent about Static for her own reasons, Hiroe bristled at the other two journalists' dismissive attitude. It was a solid service whose members knew they couldn't rest on any laurels.

"Well, if they do come, at least they won't do a hit piece on Faith Benedict and her coastal elite celebrity friends, full of dog-whistle fearmongering about aqueans," Hiroe said, smiling tightly at Riva. Perth pressed his lips together in barely contained amusement as Riva rolled her eyes.

Hiroe wasn't done. "And, you know, they'll be able to tell the story in a way a majority of people will understand, instead of doing a pompous, mind-numbing think piece that'll win awards despite no one making it through the whole thing."

Perth yawned theatrically. "Someone's got a chip on her shoulder tonight. What, are *you* gunning for a job at Static?"

Fat chance. She mumbled something and they brushed off her cutting comments and moved on to other industry gossip. Perth shamelessly eyed Riva's cleavage and she laid it on thick for the hell of it, twisting a lock of blond hair and pursing her lips in a pretty pout while listening to him.

Hiroe barely paid attention to their bored antics; she was still stinging from Perth's unintentionally well-aimed barb about Static.

She soon excused herself. She'd never engaged in the backstabbing and one-upmanship so common in the industry. It was probably one of the reasons she'd never risen very far in the ranks herself, but that wasn't why she'd gotten into reporting. Lately she'd caught herself wondering why she had in the first place.

Of course she remembered her idealistic early days, dreaming of breaking a story that changed the world. Journalism had presented itself like a lifesaver as she cast about for purpose in high school after her first passion had died for her. She'd long since gotten through disillusionment and into a mindset of acceptance, but once in a while she felt tired of what she did.

Something about the combination of philanthropists, attention-seekers, cynical reporters, and stargazers in this room had brought that feeling to the surface. Or maybe it was the mention of Static that had done it. Or maybe the drink she'd had in the waiting station hadn't fully acclimated her body to the absolute pressure of being underwater.

Whatever it was, she decided another glass of wine would help take the feeling away.

She was nursing her third glass and feeling more relaxed and content when a musical tone cut through the chatter. All eyes turned to the center of the room, where a life-sized image of Faith Benedict slowly resolved until it looked every bit as solid as the guests. The gradual appearance was for dramatic effect; there was no reason it couldn't have appeared fully formed in an instant.

The striking hologram wore what looked like a rich velvet pantsuit, all black with black embroidery creating a subtle pattern around the neck and cuffs. Her shimmering silver hair was swept back from her face in a smooth bun that swirled in a coil like a nautilus shell.

No matter where anyone was positioned in the room, Faith appeared to be facing them directly. The figure stood serenely, hands folded in front of her, until the resolution was complete and the guests had lapsed into attentive silence.

"My friends and honored guests," Faith said, "it's such a privilege to serve as your host this weekend. This event was thrown together hastily, as you know from your last-minute invitations, so I apologize for our less-than-perfect preparations. I appreciate you all making time in your busy lives despite the short notice. That tells me that this cause is every bit as urgent to you as it is to me.

"After seeing our government repeatedly fail to adequately address this health crisis for some of Earth's most vulnerable inhabitants, I decided action was needed. Not in six months, not next year, but now."

The room burst into applause and the apparition waited, nodding, until they'd quieted again. "I thank those of you who donated generously to attend this weekend's event, and your money will be put to immediate use in research and treatment.

"But that's only one of the goals I had in bringing you here, so if you came here by another means, don't think your presence isn't vital as well. I hope that by the end, after the speeches, presentations, and workshops featuring some of the best minds in the world, you'll come away with a renewed determination. That, filled with purpose, you'll spread the word, put pressure on our elected officials, and help change hearts and minds of people who think this cause, and these people, unworthy of attention and assistance."

Hiroe applauded with everyone else, clinking her rings against her champagne flute. She stole a glance at the two aquean bartenders, who were also clapping with their long-fingered webbed hands. She thought she saw tears shining in the young woman's amber eyes.

CHAPTER FIVE

The doors of the room opened and the crowd began to move toward them. Hiroe took one more glass of champagne and followed the rest of the guests.

They entered a large hallway with a moving floor. They stepped on in groups and were carried smoothly past convincing replicas of large traditional paintings and digital art displays. Hiroe found herself behind a gaggle of excited lottery winners and listened to their urgent whispered conversation with benign amusement now that the wine had mellowed her mood.

The walkway led to another door. An attendant opened it and they were at the back of an auditorium with perhaps two hundred seats, sloping down toward a dark empty stage. There was ample standing room in the back, and some of the guests remained there, milling and chatting, while others began to fill the seats.

Hiroe stood at the very back, taking it all in. The room must have been its own structure, the hallway one of the connecting tunnels. Like in the foyer of the home, the walls contained floor-to-ceiling windows, and she was once again reminded with a jolt that she was far underwater. Gardens and sea life, artfully lit, seeming to move in concert with the music that permeated the auditorium, created dazzling vistas in every direction.

"You going through a midlife crisis?" An instantly familiar voice close to her brought her out of her near hypnotic state. She turned, already rolling her eyes, to face the speaker.

"Nice to see you too, Demonte," she said.

The man continued as if she hadn't said anything. "Covering an event under the ocean? Why would you agree to this unless you decided you needed to face your fears or some shit? Prove something to yourself? Am I wrong?"

"You're wrong," she said. "I was given the assignment, so I came. That's all there is to it." She shrugged, attempting nonchalance. "Besides, if you don't look out the windows you can't even tell we're in water. It's not like we're deep sea diving."

Demonte grinned, irritatingly handsome still. His face didn't hide his age, but somehow he wore his mid-sixties in a confident, comfortable way that even Hiroe had to admit was working for him. "Well, you seem to be doing great. Congratulations." He held out his arms and Hiroe acquiesced to a short, stiff hug.

"I'm surprised to see you here, too," she said. "Don't you have a media empire to run? This is more an assignment for a beat reporter like me."

He shrugged, seemingly impervious to her sarcasm. "Static's a flat organization. Everyone contributes. Besides, I like to keep my hand in it. This is what I chose this career to do."

"Cover a rich old lady's garden party while she pays lip service to caring about the poor unfortunate aquean masses?" Hiroe shot back.

He laughed. "I missed you, Hiroe." She knew he was being sarcastic and it stung. They'd been an inseparable duo, practically able to read one another's minds, and then he was suddenly gone. She'd learned to work alone and with other reporters, but some of the pleasure had been drained from her job, and she'd never quite forgiven him for it, even ten years later.

Demonte started to say something else, but the music suddenly quieted and a hush fell over the audience. The lights outside the windows dimmed, so that only shadows of fish and waving seaweed were visible. Then the glass panels became opaque. The inside lights also came down, and the stage slowly illuminated. As it did, the figure standing in the middle also appeared on each of the windows around the audience, at varying angles and degrees of close-up. One panel to Hiroe's left was zoomed in tightly, the face filling the entire screen, and her stomach fluttered a little as the light slowly revealed its features.

The aquean man's eyes were closed. His silvery blue hair, roughly cropped in a short cut that framed his youthful face, shone in the stage lights. His eyebrows and eyelashes had the same glimmer as his hair. Mesmerized, Hiroe watched a muscle jump almost imperceptibly in the impossibly smooth, flawless green skin of his cheek as he clenched and released his jaw.

At last he opened his eyes, which were a dark amber, almost brown, and he seemed to be looking straight at her from the window panel. She looked away for a second, feeling as self-conscious as after she'd touched the VR aquean swimmer, then looked toward the stage where the man actually stood.

His blue-green lips parted and he took a deep breath. The sound that came from him was somewhere between humming and talking. Hiroe had never heard anything like it. It started deep in his throat and moved toward the front of his mouth, becoming a series of whispers, and then moved back again, returning to a more guttural sound.

She suddenly thought back to the ceremonies she'd witnessed in the VR exhibit, and thought she could begin to hear similarities to this performance. Without the distortion of traveling through water instead of air, it sounded wildly different. Also, the ceremonial singing had been joyful, and what she was hearing now was full of mourning, heartbreak, and anger.

The song, or poem, or whatever it was, seemed to reverberate inside Hiroe, creating a warmth that spread from her belly into every part of her body. She shivered, glanced around and caught Demonte watching her with a wry smile.

Hiroe stiffened and looked away haughtily. She watched the young man on the stage with folded arms, trying not to let his hypnotic performance overtake her senses again.

His vocalizing reached a crescendo that drew gasps from the audience, then cut off suddenly. The room burst into applause. He stood still with eyes downturned until it died away. Then he looked up and spoke, in English this time.

"That song is in an ancient aquean language, a language that fewer and fewer of our children are learning. The language is ancient but the song is new, written just five years ago by our most revered poet of modern times." He spoke her name in aquean, a series of sounds unreplicable by most humans.

"If you know of her, you probably know her by the human version of her name, Marteer Cosa. She wrote that lament as she lay dying of aquamycosis. She passed on shortly after. By the time she finished writing it, she was no longer able to sing it herself." His eyes pooled with liquid and Hiroe felt a lump in her throat despite her best efforts to remain unmoved.

"The song is about our stolen world," the young man continued. "It's about the death of our oceans which has sent many of us onto the land. It's about being refugees, even though we're the original people of Earth. As I'm sure you know, science has proven that we aqueans were made entirely of the Earth's elements, while humans evolved from matter that came to Earth from outer space."

He drew a breath. "The surface of our world used to be seventy-five percent ocean. Now it's eighty percent. And yet you call it Earth, for the twenty percent of the planet that is the domain of the humans. Terre, Aarde, Jorden; in almost every human language the name of our planet means 'earth.'

"But I digress," he continued. "We lost Marteer Cosa to aquamycosis as we have lost so many others; as we have lost our home, our waters, our sacred places, to the ravages of the climate crisis and the machinations of heartless corporations and governments greedy for our territory. The past decade in particular has been a period of nearly incomprehensible loss for aqueans. We thought we knew how to be resilient, but we are being tested to our very limits. We may not be able to survive this latest test."

There were rustling sounds as some audience members shifted uncomfortably in their seats, but there were also murmurs of agreement and empathy.

"I know these truths aren't easy to hear. Most would prefer to turn away from them. That's why I'm grateful to Faith Benedict, and to all of you who have come a long way, and given a great deal, in order to come and hear them. I've been losing hope. But this gathering awakens a glimmer of promise in me. Perhaps we, all of us together, can begin to bend the arc of history back toward justice for us aqueans."

He bowed deeply and turned his back, walking quickly toward the back of the stage, out of the spotlight and out of sight before the audience had a chance to realize he was done and start clapping again.

The image of Faith Benedict shimmered into convincing solidity in his place on stage. "As most of you know, that was Louvin Interre, the rising poet, historian, and aquean rights activist. I'm deeply honored by his presence here tonight, as I hope you are." The audience burst into another round of applause.

"What's with the Oz act?" Demonte muttered to Hiroe. "Why hasn't she come to her own party yet?"

"Planning a dramatic entrance later, I guess," Hiroe said with a shrug, though she'd been wondering that herself.

The hologram continued. "Next I want to welcome to the stage—" Her voice suddenly sputtered and cut off, though her image continued to mouth words. The audience stirred and whispered. Then came a crackling sound and a woman's voice cut in and out, finally coming in clearly from somewhere.

"Help me," the voice said, shakily. Then it rose to a sudden shriek. "Help me, please!"

CHAPTER SIX

For a few moments all Hiroe could hear was ragged breathing. Then: "They're trying to …" The sound cut completely and the auditorium erupted with questioning cries and worried murmurs. Some audience members stood up and looked around for the source of the voice. Hiroe hadn't seen anyone emerge when Faith had been interrupted. It was coming from somewhere else.

The image of Faith dissipated quickly from the stage. "Is this part of the show?" Demonte murmured. Hiroe didn't answer. She was already moving briskly down the middle aisle toward the stage, where she'd spotted a couple of people identically dressed, as if in some kind of uniform, leaning together and talking urgently. One of them lifted her wrist and spoke into it as Hiroe approached.

"What's going on?" Hiroe called as she got closer. The two guards looked up sharply.

"Please return to your seat, ma'am," the woman said in a terse, dismissive voice. "Everything is under control."

Hiroe started to argue but noticed the other guard held a palm-sized stun gun casually at his side. She glanced behind her and found an empty seat, perching on it, to appear to comply. By the other side of the stage, she saw the stocky man in the cheap suit who'd been staked out near the basketball star at the cocktail party. Lottie's husband Ben. He was speaking urgently to a guard who, after a moment, nodded and gestured for the man to follow him. He did so at a hurried clip.

The lights in the auditorium came up halfway, and a man walked to the edge of the stage. He held up his hand and his voice rang out over the sound system. "Ladies and gentlemen, may I please have your attention!"

The crowd's babbling subsided as everyone's eyes turned to the man.

"Thank you," he said when he was satisfied with the noise level. "Mrs. Benedict asked me to pass along her apologies for the interruption. We've investigated what you heard earlier, and we discovered the source of the voice.

"One of our guests, Lottie Wineman, wandered off to another part of the home instead of coming to the auditorium with the rest of you. Unfortunately she tripped and fell from a balcony onto the floor below. Her leg was broken."

A brief hubbub arose, but the man's raised hand once again quieted it. "She bravely crawled to a security station outside the room where she fell, and managed to activate an emergency broadcast mechanism to ask for help. Once we detected the source of the distress call, we found her there, unconscious from shock. She's been transported to Mrs.

Benedict's infirmary, where she's receiving the best of care. She'll need to stay there for the next couple of days, but we're thankful her injuries weren't more serious.

"So, without further delay, we'll continue the night's events. Up next is Doctor Stuart Hauser, one of the leading researchers in the field, to tell us more about aquamycosis and share the latest developments in our search for the cure."

Hiroe puzzled uneasily over the explanation for Lottie's transmission as a short, balding man came onto the stage to a round of applause. From her front row seat Hiroe could see his hands trembling ever so slightly. He chuckled nervously. "Well, how can I follow that excitement?" The crowd tittered politely, partly in relief. He pointed sideways with a small pen-shaped object and an image of an aquean body appeared. He moved his hand and the image zoomed in until the audience was looking at a representation of cells.

"Who are *they*?" a voice whispered next to Hiroe as the man on stage began to speak.

Startled, she turned. Her heart skipped a beat as she recognized the young aquean poet who had opened the program, and who had taken the seat next to her unnoticed. Louvin Interre. He was even more stunning up close, so much so that she found herself alternating between staring and dropping her eyes to avoid looking at him.

"Um, what?" Hiroe found her voice, inwardly mocking herself for letting a mere boy have such an effect on her.

He stood and cocked his head toward the side aisle of the auditorium. She rose and followed him as he walked quickly and quietly up toward the doors at the back of the room and out into the hallway.

There he leaned against the wall. He was dressed in loose, light-colored pants and a baggy shirt; his feet were in sandals. She hadn't even noticed how casually he'd been dressed when he was on stage, his presence and performance had been so captivating. He carried a shapeless, bulging rucksack that hung from a strap over his shoulder and across his chest.

"I saw you get shut down by security," he told her. "Did you get anything out of them?"

She shook her head. "They wouldn't even talk to me. What did you say earlier?"

"I asked what she meant by 'they,'" Louvin replied. "Did you hear what that lady said, right before the sound cut out?"

Hiroe replayed it in her mind. The young man didn't wait for her to reply. "She started to say 'they're' trying to—I don't know, do something." Now he did wait, watching Hiroe until he saw understanding dawn on her face. "If she was alone at a security station, trying to call for help, who were 'they' and what were 'they' trying to do to her?"

She tore her eyes from his mesmerizing face and looked at the ground again, shaking her head as her mind raced. He was right; it didn't fit with the official explanation. She looked up. "What do you think?"

He grimaced. "I don't know, but I do know there's something going on that they're not telling us."

"And what made you decide to tell me about it?" she asked.

"Because you were the only person trying to get information in there," he said. "Everyone else was milling around like a scattered school of fish. And because"—his eyes suddenly looked much older than the rest of him—"if I'm going to go snooping around where I'm not supposed to go, I'd like to have a human with me. Adds respectability, you know? Things'll go better if someone catches me."

Hiroe scoffed. "You don't really think security here would treat you—that's ridiculous. You're a VIP here!"

Now Louvin looked mildly disgusted, and it bothered her more than she would have thought possible. She thought she'd long ago stopped caring what people thought of her, but she felt a pang of shame.

"You don't believe me. Shocking," he said with quiet but bitter sarcasm. "Well, I don't have time to convince you that bigotry is a real thing, so … does that mean you won't come with me or what?"

"I didn't say that," Hiroe shot back. "Where are you planning to go, anyway?"

"The infirmary, to try and find out what really happened to that lady. I think I can find it—the speakers who got here early today got a tour. We didn't actually go into the building but the guide pointed it out."

Hiroe hesitated, but she already knew she was deciding to do it. She'd miss part of the program, possibly get kicked out of the estate (although no one had expressly forbidden guests to explore the place, so she thought that was unlikely). But she was charmed by the idea of playing a fiftysomething Nancy Drew in a giant mansion.

And she couldn't shake the thought that something else really was going on. Lottie hadn't sounded in pain to her on the sound system—she'd sounded terrified. And when she'd stopped talking, it didn't sound like she'd fallen unconscious so much as been interrupted. Possibly by someone else turning off the microphone.

And, Hiroe reluctantly admitted to herself, she didn't mind being close to Louvin. It was ridiculous, but his effect on her was undeniable. Even Demonte had noticed it, much to her chagrin.

"I'm a reporter. I can't pass up a chance for a story," she said with a little laugh. She liked the way his eyes lit up, like a little kid who just talked his way into getting some candy.

CHAPTER SEVEN

The moving walkway automatically came to life in the other direction as they started making their way down the hall. Louvin stepped off it halfway toward the main house, into an alcove with a door, and Hiroe followed his lead.

Once on the other side of the door, her heart sank. She recognized the capsule as similar to the one she'd taken from the surface down to the estate. "No tunnel to the infirmary, huh?" she said.

Louvin shook his head. "There might be, but this was the way they took me on the tour." He opened the door with a tap and held out a hand as if to help Hiroe in. She felt a flash of indignation despite her trepidation and brushed aside his assistance, climbing in on her own. He followed her in and pressed the button to close the door.

The interior was comfortable but small. The seats were close enough together that their elbows brushed against each other whenever one of them shifted even slightly. "Let's see if I can figure this out," Louvin said with a grin. He tapped the control screen lightly. It didn't take long for him to find and request the infirmary as their destination.

The craft barely made a sound as it left its dock and slid into a tunnel that sloped down into water. They were out in the ocean in less than thirty seconds. Hiroe gripped the sides of her seat; she hadn't been prepared to face this again so soon.

"You okay?" Louvin asked with solicitous concern, and her irritation helped overcome her stress.

"Fine, I'm fine," she muttered. "I'm not some delicate old lady. You don't have to treat me like I'm fragile."

"I didn't mean to do that," Louvin said with a shrug. She felt slightly embarrassed for her outburst. "It's just a couple of minutes away."

He didn't need to tell her that. The screen showed their progress and their estimated arrival. She kept her eyes glued on it and focused on keeping her breathing steady. "So," she said, trying to take her mind off her fear, "do you think Faith Benedict is as devoted to this cause as she makes it seem?"

Louvin glanced at her with a sly half smile. "You're a reporter, right? On the record, Faith Benedict is the most devoted human to the cause of aquean rights and aquamycosis eradication there is."

"And off the record? You think it's just for show? Something she can pat herself on the back about? Maybe to justify building her home so close to the Infinite Water Trench?"

"Wow, Ms. Reporter, those are what I'd call some leading questions," he said with a teasing note in his voice. Then he turned serious. "Look, I don't pretend to know anyone's true motivations—no one does. All we can do is assess people by their actions. And I don't know anyone—human or aquean—I approve of one hundred percent. But if you look at the totality of Faith's actions, she's done more for aquamycosis awareness and research than any other human who's not a scientist or a doctor."

The silence between them began to grow again but was interrupted again, this time by the craft.

The progress map on the screen was replaced with a black circle. A female voice said, "Please confirm identity to continue." An illustration of a hand appeared and animated to show the thumb pressing a black circle similar to the large one in the middle of the screen. Hiroe and Louvin's eyes met, surprised.

Louvin shrugged and pressed his thumb against the screen. It beeped and flashed red. "Please try again. Please confirm identity to continue." Hiroe looked outside and realized the craft was slowing.

"What's happening?" she said, trying to stifle the instant alarm she felt.

"I don't know. Maybe it doesn't recognize aquean fingers or something. Try yours," Louvin said tensely.

Hiroe reached for the screen and pressed her thumb against it. Her heart sank as the screen reacted the exact same way.

"Are you a guest?" the voice inquired sweetly.

"Yes," Louvin and Hiroe said simultaneously.

"Please enter your guest code to continue," the voice said. A numerical touchpad now replaced the black circle.

"Did you get a guest code?" Hiroe hissed.

Louvin shook his head. "Why is it only asking now?" he said in frustration. "Why did it let us get started?" The craft had now drifted to a stop and settled on the ocean floor. They were in the middle of one of the typically well-tended aquatic gardens, but the lacy seaweed and staring fish surrounding them now felt oppressive instead of picturesque.

"Fuck!" Louvin slammed the heel of his hand on the screen. The voice came back on.

"Do you want to call for assistance?"

"Yes," Hiroe said. Louvin glared at her but didn't say anything. The screen flickered.

"I'm sorry, I didn't get that. Do you want to call for assistance?"

"Yes!" There was a hectic edge to Hiroe's voice this time. Her chest began to tighten and she started to breathe too fast.

"I'm sorry, I didn't get ..." the voice became sluggish and stopped. The craft shuddered. With almost a sigh, the door unsealed and slid open. Air escaped in a rush of bubbles as water pushed its way in with sudden force.

Hiroe's uncontrollably fast shallow breathing didn't allow her to fill her lungs with fresh air before the water was upon her. Her throat closed before her mouth; she looked wildly around, her eyes stinging from the salt water. The seatbelt hadn't released and she clawed at it, unable to find a button or buckle.

Her panic began to be replaced with a heavy dread as she recognized the futility of her efforts. Her lungs were already burning, black spots swimming in front of her eyes. She wondered how long it would be until her throat surrendered and allowed the ocean to take full possession of her body.

Her hands fell away from the seatbelt and she curled up as tightly as she could in the seat, burying her face in her arms. Her head swam and she squeezed her eyes shut.

So she would finally find out how it felt. It was long overdue.

CHAPTER EIGHT

Hiroe had been swimming since she was an infant, essentially, and had Olympic dreams. She trained to become fast and competitive, but her real love was spending long periods of time in the water, especially underwater.

Her parents were fond of island vacations and she spent most of her time snorkeling or diving on every trip. She often thought if her competitive swim career didn't pan out, she'd end up a scuba instructor or tour guide.

So it was especially exciting when her school swim team took a field trip to go diving off the coast of Mexico for three days. Her best friend Elise had listened to her tales of previous vacations with envy, and Hiroe was looking forward to showing off her knowledge. She promised to take her somewhere special that only the two of them would get to see.

On the first day of the trip, the team did a series of guided dives in a highly populated area. Hiroe stifled her impatience, but that night she and Elise got worked up planning their adventure, and she started the second day more determined than ever to give her friend a one-of-a-kind experience.

That morning they were allowed to explore a designated underwater area with buddies, and she and Elise paired off. It was pretty but didn't satisfy their need for excitement. As soon as their coaches and the instructors were occupied with other pairs, the girls swam off from the group.

A tunnel rimmed with waving anemones beckoned them on. They swam together, past stunning rock formations and strange sea life. The tunnel swooped and turned a few times, and they followed happily, wondering where it would come out.

They turned a corner and it dropped downward into darkness. Hiroe, flush with excitement from their adventure so far, tugged on Elise's hand. She saw the girl's hesitation on her face but wordlessly coaxed her into following.

Almost immediately they were lost. Bumping against walls and one another, they panicked and lost their sense of direction. Then Hiroe didn't feel Elise bumping against her anymore. She swam wildly, scraping her arms and legs against the walls of the tunnel as she flailed to find Elise. She thought she felt her air supply dwindling and started to give up on ever finding her way out.

Then she saw a grayish blue hue in the water. A hint of daylight. She swam toward it until she reached familiar scenery, but Elise wasn't there and didn't follow. Hiroe clawed her way back to the rest of the group. Search parties found Elise later that day, trapped near the dark dead end, her foot wedged between two rocks.

* * *

Something touched her cheeks, then gripped the sides of her head. She opened her eyes and stared uncomprehending at Louvin, whose own face was just inches away from hers. She'd forgotten where she was.

He came even closer to her and his lips touched hers, which were clamped tightly together. She felt something light on her mouth, spreading around it, a widening area that grew to encompass her nose as well. Louvin drew slowly away from her. She saw him mouth a word: Breathe.

Her burning lungs obeyed, though it made no sense. She exhaled a little stale air first, then inhaled, expecting water to flow into her mouth and nose.

It did not. She breathed air. She gasped raggedly and her body greedily demanded more and more oxygen. Louvin leaned toward her again and did something again, not touching her lips this time. She glanced down and thought she saw the edge of some kind of bubble or clear sphere covering her nose.

Louvin spoke in her ear, his voice sounding muffled in the water. "Try not to take such deep breaths; it'll last longer." He reached behind him to an outer pocket of his rucksack and withdrew a knife. He cut her seatbelt easily, then his. He left the capsule, and turned with his hand outstretched to make sure Hiroe was following him.

She was not. She sat frozen in her seat. Louvin ducked back into the capsule and pulled her out by her shoulders. She actually struggled at first, her breath quickening, but he put his arms around her and held her close against him. Something about the solidity and slight warmth of his body compared with the water made her feel safer. She stopped struggling and he refilled her air supply. Then he pulled her from the car.

Her limbs still felt frozen with fear, but Louvin kept his arm wrapped around her slender frame. She could feel his powerful kicks as he propelled them through the water.

She began to feel hope that they would survive, but wondered how they would reach safety. She was completely disoriented and lost.

Louvin seemed to swim with purpose, though, and she soon saw what he was aiming for: one of the tunnels connecting two buildings. She realized it was raised off the ocean floor about four feet, and as they approached, Louvin dove lower.

As he brought them close to the ocean floor and swam under the tunnel, Hiroe squeezed her eyes shut again, a wave of claustrophobic fear rushing over her again. She felt Louvin straining to do something and opened them again cautiously.

He'd found a circular seam on the underside of the tunnel, like a portal. With the arm that wasn't holding her fast against him, he alternated banging it with his fist and running his hand around it to look for a latch or button that would open it.

Hiroe felt the edge of her air bubble touching the tip of her nose, getting close to her mouth as it filtered out her exhalations and she depleted the breathable air within it. She elbowed Louvin—it was the only way she could think of to get his attention in the awkward position she was in.

He stopped trying to open the hatch and focused for a few moments on replenishing her oxygen supply. Even in the midst of oppressive terror, she felt a wave of gratitude as her lungs once again filled with air.

Louvin redoubled his efforts, but he appeared to be making no progress. She saw his jaw muscles tense. He looked around as if considering swimming somewhere else. She wondered how long he was able to breathe underwater while sharing his air with her, and a pang of guilt cut through her fear. She wanted to ask him. She said his name but the bubble and water muffled her voice and his pounding on the tunnel drowned it out.

He paused again to check on her, then reached in his shoulder bag—possibly searching for the knife he'd used earlier, she guessed, but he came up empty.

He'd managed to look admirably calm up until now, but she could see desperation dawning in his eyes. Her own temporary hope had all but dissipated by now. Would she die like this, locked in his arm? Would he find his way to safety? If not, when would their bodies be found?

She didn't want to cause his underwater death, even if she wouldn't be around to shoulder the guilt. She tried to tell him to leave her, struggling weakly to get away, but he didn't seem to hear her or notice her trying to break free.

She felt her eyelids growing heavy. Reality receded. She couldn't tell if she was going into shock, fainting from the stress, or dying. In any case she couldn't move her limbs anymore. She gave up and closed her eyes. *I didn't deserve to live this long,* she thought.

Suddenly the arm around her waist tightened, and she was being pulled upward.

CHAPTER NINE

Hiroe's eyes opened to see the circular portal gone and light shining through the hole it had left. By the time she'd taken that in, Louvin had hauled her halfway out of the water, and she collapsed face down on the floor of the tunnel. The lifesaving bubble evaporated from her face and she breathed deeply for the first time in several minutes.

Her legs were still submerged in water. She wasn't sure why it didn't flood the chamber she was in, but she didn't have the energy to ponder it for long. She struggled to crawl the rest of the way through the opening, and rested as soon as she was all the way in. Her clothes felt heavy, and her short bobbed hair was plastered against her skull.

"Villanna!" Louvin said with surprise, and Hiroe sat up and turned to look at him. She saw with a little shock that he was now standing beside the portal holding the hands of a stunning young aquean woman.

The woman gave him a bright joyful smile, but she pulled her hands away and knelt on the floor. "Just a second, Louvin," she said. She wrestled with the round plate and latched it in place over the portal. Then she stood and threw herself into his arms.

Hiroe watched with an unidentifiable pang. She couldn't remember the last time she'd felt romantic jealousy. That wasn't what this was, not exactly, but she felt foolish about her attraction to him as the two beautiful creatures clung to one another.

Finally they withdrew from the embrace and Hiroe tried to affix a smile onto her face, or at least a neutral expression. "Thank you for saving us," she said to the girl. Villanna's smile broadened even more.

"I heard you out there," she said. "I mean"—she looked back at Louvin—"I heard *you.*"

Louvin was grinning. "I didn't even think about that," he told the girl. "Everything happened so suddenly, I was just trying to get in by myself."

"It was so faint, I was lucky I could find you," she replied. "I'm glad you're all right."

"I'm fine, but I don't know how long I could have kept—I'm sorry ..." He looked over at Hiroe, and she said her name, not able to remember if she'd ever even introduced herself to him. "—kept Hiroe alive." His face looked haunted for a moment as if reliving the last few minutes in the water.

Villanna turned toward Hiroe. "I'm glad there was a little bit of my connection to this loser left over from when we were kids," she said, jerking her thumb at Louvin with a dismissive gesture. "Hi Hiroe, I'm Villanna." She bent forward and stretched a delicately webbed hand with slender fingers toward Hiroe. "I'm his sister."

Their hands clasped, and then Hiroe was pulled to her feet with a surprisingly strong tug given the girl's waifish appearance. No giant herself, Hiroe nevertheless felt gawky once she was standing next to Villanna.

"So you, what? Have some kind of psychic connection?" Hiroe asked.

Villanna shrugged. "There's probably some scientific explanation for it, but my people aren't interested in being studied like lab rats about something that doesn't need to be explained. All aquean kids can tell when our siblings are in trouble, within a certain distance at least. It wears off—or at least, should've worn off—by our early twenties."

Hiroe nodded, fascinated, but something else occurred to her before she could question that. "And what about the—" she made a curved shape like a bubble with her hand in front of her face. "Is that something every aquean can do?"

"Oh, yeah," Louvin said. "Well, I'd heard of it being done, but I'd never had a reason to try it myself, so I'm glad it worked."

"It's incredible," Hiroe said.

"Yeah, it's a trick we developed as we started interacting more with humans. We can get our oxygen from water, so we can concentrate it like that, and the bubble—sorry, this is gonna sound gross—is mucus. It's not ideal air for humans, though. You shouldn't have any side effects or anything now that you're breathing normal air again, but I wasn't sure how long it would keep you going."

"Well, thank you, both of you. Again." She frowned. "I wonder what happened to the thing we were riding in?"

Louvin shook his head. "Kind of scary that it doesn't have any fail-safe mechanism, safety equipment, or anything."

"Actually," Villanna said, "if you were using one of the water cars, they all have scuba gear stored inside them."

Louvin looked stricken. "Holy shit," he said. He turned to Hiroe. "I'm so, so sorry. I can't believe I risked your life like that when I could have—"

She waved her hand and cut him off. "Don't even. It's not like I knew that equipment was there either, so I'd have died for sure if I'd been in there alone. You saved me. Period." She turned her attention back to Villanna. "Did you two come here together?"

The girl looked surprised, then laughed. "Oh, no! No, I actually work here. I'm Mrs. Benedict's nurse—well, one of them."

"My sister decided to sell out and work for not only a human, but one of the richest humans in the world," Louvin broke in.

Villanna's beautiful golden eyes flashed with annoyance. "Oh, and what are you doing here? Working for free?"

"I'm not doing this for the money," Louvin shot back.

"But I bet you didn't turn it down."

Hiroe knew the beginnings of an endless sibling fight when she saw one and broke in. "So do you know about the guest who broke her leg?"

That did the trick. They instantly forgot their argument. "What did you say?" Villanna asked.

Louvin explained why they were there. Villanna's face cleared. "No, yeah, that lady's in the infirmary. She's fine. I think the weird thing she said must've been because she was going into shock from the pain." She looked pityingly at them. "Shame you almost died for nothing."

Hiroe felt a mix of disappointment and relief at the news. "Lesson learned, I guess?" she said. "Any idea what we should do about the car we trashed?"

Villanna waved her hand. "Don't worry about it. She's got a garage full of them. Besides, obviously something was already wrong with it if it let you guys start it without a code. I'll call someone from maintenance to get it."

"Thanks," Hiroe said, relieved. "You'd think I'm old enough to know better than to run around taking stupid chances, but ..." She laughed ruefully. "I guess we should get back to the auditorium, huh?"

Louvin nodded reluctantly. "You coming, sis?"

"Can't," said Villanna. "I'm on duty."

"Oh yeah, that reminds me," said Hiroe. "Is Faith okay? We haven't seen her yet—at least, not in person."

"Yeah, she's okay," Villanna said. "Probably waiting until later to make her official entrance, for dramatic effect or whatever."

"That's what I figured," Hiroe said.

Louvin looked unwilling to let go of his theory that something was being covered up about the lottery winner's mysterious transmission, but when Hiroe turned to go—after asking Villanna for a way back that wouldn't involve getting in the water—he followed her.

CHAPTER TEN

They traveled along a tunnel with no moving walkway for several minutes. Hiroe felt her breathing become more labored.

She masked the sound of it as best she could. "At least our clothes might be mostly dry by the time we get back," she said, only sounding partly out of breath.

The tunnel ended at a door. Louvin held it open and Hiroe strode through, attempting to move briskly.

They seemed to be in the main home, judging from the finishes made to look like wood and velvet that reminded her of decor she'd seen earlier. Or it was just another outbuilding decorated to match the main one.

She felt lightheaded. She attempted to push through the feeling by quickening her pace, but her feet tangled together and she fell forward. Her hands instinctively reached out and broke her fall, which kept her face from hitting the floor. Luckily it was carpeted so her palms only suffered a rug burn.

She rolled over and lay for a second, frustrated and disoriented. Suddenly Louvin's pale green face was above her. Her cheeks burned and she attempted to stand. As soon as she did, a headrush threatened to topple her again. This time he caught her in his arms and lifted her off the floor.

She felt humiliated but held onto his shoulder with one arm so she wasn't completely limp. He carried her, with little apparent effort, through a faux but convincing mahogany door and into a room decorated like a study in some Victorian period piece. The walls were made to look like dark wood and the furnishings, like the chaise lounge Louvin laid her on, looked and felt like velvet.

The walls were lined with bookshelves containing what appeared to be real paper books. It seemed risky to Hiroe to keep such belongings underwater, even though the mansion was watertight. Hiroe found herself wondering in her lightheaded state what Louvin's people read, those who were still in the ocean, living underwater and in damp subterranean caves. Would books survive those conditions?

She realized he was watching her closely, his face tense and worried, and attempted again to snap out of it. She sat up a little. "Fuck!" she said to try and break the heavy silence. She attempted a tone of humorous self-deprecation. "Guess I'm getting too old to have adventures like this."

Louvin sat on the edge of the lounge. She felt bad but somewhat gratified by how concerned he looked. "That's not it," he said. "You've been breathing the wrong kind of air for too long. And you've been through a traumatic experience. I'm sure you'll recover. You just need to rest."

He touched her hand, then took it between his after a slight hesitation. "I think we're a ways from where everything's happening. You don't have to rush things. I saw how many speakers and performers there are—this shit will go on for hours tonight, and continue tomorrow." He smiled tentatively, but she thought she saw his lower lip quiver. "Just relax. I couldn't—I don't know what I'd do if you were seriously hurt because of me."

Even in her current state, Hiroe felt a tingling warmth spreading from his hand through her body. But she pulled away and sat up a little more. "I'm fine. Really. Why don't you go back to the party? I'll come in a little bit after I rest some more." She smiled. "Go have fun. You don't want to spend the whole time looking after some old lady."

Louvin shook his head with a little laugh. "Why do you keep saying that?" he said. He reached out and touched her cheek with his fingertips. His hand strayed up and stroked her still-damp hair. "You're amazing. I'm sure you know that, but just in case you don't …"

He bent toward her and brushed his lips against the same spot on her cheek, then trailed them to her mouth and pressed against her lips. Taken by surprise, Hiroe nearly froze. Her heartbeat seemed to double in speed.

He drew back. "I mean, you're all right for a human." He surprised a laugh out of her. "I hope I didn't freak you out," he said.

"No, not at all!" Hiroe protested. "It's just the first—I mean, I've never kissed a— someone so much younger than me," she finished lamely.

It was his turn to laugh. "You can say it, it's not offensive or anything. Hell, I've never kissed a human before either."

"Really?" Hiroe felt relieved. There was a clear political divide between those who objected to human-aquean relations and those who were open-minded about it, so she'd been afraid she'd appear to be in the former category.

"Never, until now," he said. He smiled down at her. "It was good though." She melted a little inside, and he must have seen something in her eyes, because he leaned down again until their mouths were less than an inch apart. "Did you think so?" he said in a softer voice.

Hiroe couldn't muster any real will to resist, or even think of a good reason why she should try, when his eyes were searching hers with such frank interest. Instead she lifted her head to claim his lips in another kiss. Her eyes had closed, but she felt Louvin's body slowly lower onto hers until she was pinned down on the lounge. Their clothes, still damp, felt chilly against her skin at first, but they soon warmed up as their bodies pressed together.

She ran a hand under his loose shirt and felt the impossibly soft skin of his waist and back. She wondered if he always felt slightly damp or if it was just because they hadn't dried off from their ordeal. Whichever it was, it made his skin feel smooth and almost slippery.

Wherever she touched, his body, cool at first, warmed under her hand.

He slipped his hands beneath her sequined top and traced his way from her belly to the underside of her left breast. Her breath caught in her throat. It had been over a year since anyone had touched her this way. She told herself it helped explain how overwhelmed she felt.

Louvin sat up and pulled his shirt over his head, and Hiroe drank in his greenish-blue skin, like the surface of the ocean on a cloudy day. The voice telling her this wasn't her usual behavior in a strange place, or anywhere anymore, was very faint and easily disregarded. She felt in a kind of daze as he helped her stand and slip off her clothes down to her underwear.

He did the same with his own clothes and Hiroe shivered as their bodies touched. His hands, webbed about halfway up his long fingers, roamed over her body, and she imagined every inch of skin he touched became as smooth and soft as his.

Hiroe's breath came in sharp gasps. Everywhere they touched, wherever their bodies made contact, pleasure bloomed and spread across her skin, permeating her body.

Louvin's mouth locked with hers, and their tongues explored one another's mouths. His was narrower, smoother than she expected, but she relished its feel against hers, its probing insistence. She felt herself slowly being moved backward; her bare feet stepped back one at a time until she felt velvety cloth and, under that, the solidity of the wall.

Then Louvin pushed his whole body tightly against her. She would have collapsed but for the wall and for one of Louvin's arms firmly encircling her waist. She couldn't stop herself from moving against him, reacting to each wave of pleasure that his body sent into hers.

She became gradually aware that the inside of his arm around her, from slightly above the wrist to his underarm, had a different texture than the rest of his skin. She touched his other arm with her hand, ran her fingers curiously over the row of raised circular somethings. As she touched the smooth concave middle of one, it contracted around her fingertip slightly.

She gasped. She remembered now that aqueans had suction cups on their limbs similar to those on octopus tentacles. Every one she'd encountered so far tonight had been wearing long sleeves and it hadn't occurred to her before, but she found it didn't bother her. She ran her hand up and down his arm. They felt as good as the rest of him.

Louvin moved his arm away and she was worried at first that she'd hurt or annoyed him with her caresses. But then he slid his free hand under the waistband of her underwear and pushed them down so they slipped to the floor.

His fingers brushed against her and his hand continued between her legs until she was practically straddling his forearm. Another gasp escaped her as she felt her clitoris enclosed in a smooth, soft trap. The gentle movement caused a tingling sensation, an almost unbearable feeling of pure pleasure.

Hiroe clung to Louvin as the sensations began to gather intensity at her core. It built quickly and she had little time to anticipate its climax before her knees buckled.

She depended on the wall to help her stay upright as Louvin slowly released her from his embrace. She slumped against it, panting.

She suddenly felt exposed and retrieved her clothing from the nearby lounge. She felt his eyes on her as she dressed, and felt unable to stop taking peeks at his slender but muscled physique as he put his shirt back on. She already ached for the feel of his cool, fast-warming flesh on her bare skin again.

"Hey," he said. Hiroe looked up and met his eyes reluctantly. He moved toward her and gripped her waist with his whole arm again. How often had that happened just in the past hour or two, she wondered, remembering with disbelief her rescue from the water that her clothes hadn't even completely dried from yet. And everything that had happened since then.

She couldn't exactly feel the suction cups through both of their shirts but now that she knew they were there, she imagined she could detect their texture all around her midsection.

"Thanks," he whispered.

Hiroe laughed, feeling awkward. "I guess I should be the one thanking you," she said, trying to sound lighthearted. "I didn't do anything for you."

"Not yet," he said boldly, then looked unsure, as if he thought his presumption would offend her. She was flattered by his interest and oddly charmed by his combination of swagger and insecurity, but she tried to mask it.

"We should get back," she said briskly. She thought she saw a flash of disappointment on Louvin's face, but if so, it was gone almost as quickly as it had appeared. He nodded and hoisted his ever-present rucksack over his shoulder.

"Are you feeling up to walking?" he asked. "I don't know if many of the hallways over here have conveyors; I don't think I've been in this part before."

Hiroe nodded. She actually did feel recovered; whether it was adrenaline from their encounter or she was really better, she couldn't tell. "I probably look like hell, but there's nothing I can do about that," she said. She hadn't even brought a handbag; all her beauty supplies were in the suitcase that had been taken as soon as she arrived. She ran her fingers through her pageboy in an attempt to restore order. Louvin reached out and helped her, smiling.

"You look great," he said, and she found it impossible not to return his smile.

CHAPTER ELEVEN

With a few wrong turns into dead ends, they eventually made their way back to the main part of the house where the large gathering spaces were.

They found the foyer and from there the moving walkway to the auditorium. Others were emerging from various rooms and hallways and taking the conveyor back with them, so they blended in quite well. The clumps of people in front of and behind them were chatting animatedly, but Hiroe and Louvin were silent, lost in their separate thoughts.

In the auditorium, Hiroe spotted Demonte almost immediately, standing in the back. She had a sudden visceral desire that he not detect anything between her and the poet. She stopped and Louvin hesitated, giving her a questioning look. "Well, see you later," she said in a bright voice that didn't sound like her own. He hunched his shoulders a little and she felt a pang of pity. But he straightened and flashed a confident grin.

"Okay, bye," he said, and continued down the aisle. She feasted her eyes on his tall slender frame once more, then looked away—directly at Demonte, who was watching her with an assessing manner.

"You look like hell," he said, and she laughed, then felt irritated. "What have you been up to?"

Hiroe thought about ignoring the question and trying to put him off the scent, or trying to come up with a plausible cover story. Both seemed harder than just telling him where she'd been. Anyway, nothing had come of it, so it wasn't like she had a scoop to protect.

Ever since Demonte had abruptly quit her news service to co-found Static, their old way of teasing each other had turned into outright antagonism at times, which had led her to avoid him whenever possible.

So she braced herself for Demonte to laugh at her hapless and misguided adventure, especially when she got to the part where Villanna had confirmed that Lottie really had been taken to the infirmary with a broken leg. Instead he listened with a thoughtful air, his forehead creased.

"Here's where you get to tell me I'm an asshole for going on that wild goose chase with a paranoid kid," Hiroe said preemptively.

Demonte smiled, but not in a derisive way. "Man, there's nothing I'd like more, believe me," he said. "But here's the thing." His eyes roved around the room. "Yeah, no, I'm not wrong."

"What are you talking about?" Hiroe said impatiently.

He kept scanning the room as audience members applauded for the next speaker, who had just stepped on stage. "Your friend Lottie? She's not the only one who's not here anymore."

CHAPTER TWELVE

It took a moment for Hiroe to process that. "You mean—?"

Demonte took his eyes off the crowd and looked at her. "You know I'd notice if people were missing who were here before, right?"

She did know. Demonte had a nearly photographic memory, especially for faces. It was rare in an age where practically every bit of information anyone needed was instantaneously accessible. Most people had brain-wave-controlled smart device implants, and many pundits, scientists, and philosophers bemoaned the atrophying of the human brain's memory. So Demonte's gift stood out.

And, Hiroe suddenly realized, in a setting where no recording devices were allowed, he might be the only person who'd notice a few strange faces gone from a large crowd.

"Who's gone?" she asked. "Did you meet them? Did you recognize them from somewhere else?"

"I spoke with a couple of them—sweepstakes winners, like Lottie. The others, no, but they weren't anyone well-known. My guess is they were random winners too."

"Were they all human or—"

"Yeah, just human." Demonte gave a cynical laugh. "I think I've seen maybe two aqueans that weren't waiters or public figures. I'm guessing the lottery advertising didn't target them. Surprise, surprise."

"How many are missing?" Hiroe asked.

"I don't know, a dozen, maybe?"

Hiroe's mind raced. "How could that many people go missing? They just wandered away?"

He shrugged. "Maybe. Maybe they all wanted to go exploring more than they wanted to be at the event, or got tired and went to their rooms."

She shook her head slowly. "I talked to Lottie before the program started and all she could talk about were the famous people. I heard some others talking about that too. I don't think anything would tear them away."

Demonte nodded. "Yeah, doesn't seem likely to me either."

"When did you notice?" Hiroe said.

"Just now," he said. "They put us into groups, each one with a scientist or doctor, and we had breakout sessions while you were gone. When people started coming back in, I was watching for this one cute girl." He smiled ruefully. "When she didn't come in, I started looking closer and noticed a few other faces were missing. And I kept remembering more, especially after hearing your story."

He spread his hands wide. "I guess some of them could have left before, but a few of them definitely went toward the breakout sessions and didn't come back in here afterward."

"Well, okay." Hiroe thought. "If we don't think they went to bed, what other possible explanation is there?"

"I have no idea," Demonte said. "I really don't."

Hiroe shook her head. "Me either." She looked around. "I'm going to get Louvin." She bristled at Demonte's knowing look. "He deserves to know, since he cared enough to go looking for the truth." She started toward the front of the auditorium.

"Just don't get in another underwater car with him," she heard Demonte say as she walked away. She didn't dignify that with so much as a backward glance.

She spotted Louvin near the front, got his attention and beckoned for him to follow her to the back of the room. She was somewhat surprised that he came readily after her previous brushoff.

She awkwardly introduced him to Demonte and prayed that he didn't sense anything between her and Louvin, even though every time she looked at the young aquean, scenes from the evening flashed back to her, like the feel of his arm between her legs. She remembered him helping her neaten her hair, and that flustered her even more for some reason.

But she managed to explain why she'd called him back there, and Demonte detailed what he'd noticed. Louvin, gratified that perhaps his suspicions hadn't been unfounded, went straight back into Nancy Drew mode.

"But what about your sister?" Hiroe asked. "She confirmed what they said about Lottie."

"Yeah, but did she actually see her?" Louvin asked. "Maybe she took someone else's word for it."

Hiroe searched her memory for exactly what Villanna had said. "Okay, but before we go running off wrecking cars and almost killing ourselves again, let's look through the rooms where the breakout sessions happened. And maybe instead of sneaking around, we could just ask some questions if we don't find the missing people," she said.

The program was wrapping up. The keynote speaker, a senator sympathetic to the aqueans' plight, was pontificating with increasing passion, clearly approaching the conclusion of his speech. The three of them slipped out the back door of the auditorium and Demonte led the way to a corridor of smaller conference-style rooms.

A few minutes of searching confirmed that the missing attendees weren't lingering in any of the rooms. They were all dark and empty.

As the trio headed back in the other direction, a man in a security guard uniform stepped into their path, looking imposing. Hiroe approached him purposefully.

"I hope you can help us," she said before he had a chance to say anything that would put them on the defensive. "We're looking for some people we met earlier, and they weren't in the main auditorium, so we came to see if they'd stayed behind after the breakout sessions. But they're not here either. Is there somewhere else people are gathering?"

The man didn't relax his posture, but he seemed a little less suspicious. "I don't really know anything about that," he said. "You'd have to ask someone else. You better go back to the auditorium; there are other guards there."

"Okay, thanks," Hiroe said, as if he'd said something helpful. "Hey, do you happen to know where Mrs. Benedict is? Will she be making an appearance tonight?"

"I don't have any information on that either, ma'am," he said. Hiroe felt a surge of exasperation.

Demonte broke in. "I might be feeling like turning in a little early tonight, but I didn't get shown where the sleeping quarters are. Can you point me in the right direction?"

The man looked over at him. "Look, I'm just a security guard," he said. "I'm not a tour guide and I don't have a map or guest list or agenda for the night or anything like that. Now why don't y'all head back and find someone who can help you?"

Hiroe looked back over her shoulder as they left; she saw the man talking into a ring-sized device on a finger of his right hand, but he made no attempt to follow them.

"Well, that guy's pretending to be something he isn't," Demonte murmured as they walked.

"Totally," Louvin agreed.

"What do you mean?" Hiroe asked.

"You heard him—he doesn't know anything," Louvin said. "Why would a guard not have at least a basic idea of what parts of the estate people are gathering in? Faith's security staff lives on site here, just like all her employees. No way he wouldn't at least know where the guest quarters are."

"So?" Hiroe was irritated at the men's certainty. "Maybe he's new. Maybe she hired additional security since this is such a big event. There's no way of knowing he's—" She broke off.

"What is it?" Demonte asked.

"Just now I saw him talking into a finger communicator. The other guards in the auditorium had theirs on their wrists. Could members of that team have different tech from each other?"

"Really doubtful," Demonte said "Why would they? Simpler to maintain if they use the same hardware for everyone."

Louvin's eyes gleamed with interest. "Whatever's going on, he could have something to do with it. Maybe—I don't know, maybe someone has infiltrated the estate. Maybe they're kidnapping guests. Okay, not that. Maybe the people who disappeared are spying or trying to steal something—money? Valuables? Or maybe—" he waved his hand excitedly "—medical research stuff!"

"Okay, let's not get ahead of ourselves," Demonte said. "There are just a couple of odd things we've run across. They may not have anything to do with each other. They may all have innocent explanations. Let's think about which we can clear up first."

"I wish we knew where Faith Benedict was," Hiroe said. "That's bugging me more than just about anything. None of her messages talk about her not being able to attend, so why isn't she here? It makes no sense to me."

"Okay," Louvin said musingly. "So if we could find Faith, find out why she's not attending the events, that might tell us something?" Demonte and Hiroe agreed.

"Follow me," Louvin said. He strode off and the other two followed him, exchanging puzzled glances. He turned down a hallway and into one of the breakout rooms.

"I can find Faith," he said. He lifted the strap of his bag off his shoulder and set it on a chair.

CHAPTER THIRTEEN

Louvin knelt by his bag and unfastened it carefully. Hiroe hadn't seen him open the main compartment before, just some of the outer pockets. Something about the way he was handling it made her step closer and look inside.

She wasn't sure what she was seeing. The bag appeared to be full of a bright yellow, solid yet somehow stringy, wet-looking substance. She met Louvin's eyes and he could see her confusion.

"Meet my best friend," he said. "Bruno, this is Hiroe. Hiroe, Bruno."

"Um," Hiroe stalled, not sure if it was some sort of joke. "Okay …"

"I know how it must sound, but I'm not kidding," Louvin said. "I can tell you all about it sometime, but right now we should be trying to find Faith. Bruno can find people." He reached down and touched the yellow mass. His hand started to sink into it; Hiroe couldn't tell if he was pushing the substance aside or if the thing was moving to accommodate him. Soon his hand was submerged up to his wrist.

His eyes closed. His lips moved almost imperceptibly as if he were talking to himself, but no sound emerged. At one point he smiled as if to himself. "Later, I'll tell you later," he whispered. After a pause he chuckled, then assumed a more serious expression.

Hiroe and Demonte exchanged glances, both of them suddenly dubious about their new acquaintance but also fascinated by the sight before them, even if it made no sense.

A couple minutes seemed to stretch out like an eternity in the small quiet room. Finally Louvin withdrew his hand slowly, refastened the bag, and stood up, shouldering it. "Okay," he said. "I think I got it." He wouldn't elaborate, but he sounded confident that he'd learned something, so the reporters went along with it in the absence of any other leads.

They split up. Demonte went back to rejoin the other guests, who according to the program were scheduled to be leaving the auditorium for another cocktail reception in the ballroom before the program ended for the night. He'd keep an eye out for more people disappearing, or any missing guests coming back, while Louvin and Hiroe went in search of Faith.

Left alone once again with Louvin, but not entirely alone, she realized, Hiroe struggled to find anything to say. They walked, then rode moving walkways, in silence for a while.

Finally she broke it. "So can, um, Bruno hear me right now?"

"Sort of," Louvin said. "It doesn't have ears, so not in the way you would think of hearing, but it has a sense of what's happening. It's told me that if it's not focusing, things can be distant and hard to understand. I guess like sound being muffled, or like your vision being blurry. Except it doesn't have eyes either, so not exactly like that either."

"Hmm," Hiroe said. "So after we left your sister, when we were in that room …" She trailed off, but the question was clear.

"Oh," Louvin said, looking abashed but slightly amused. "Well, yes, it was sort of aware, but … Bruno's whole way of looking at things, it's not the same as humans or aqueans. So it's not like if a person was in the room with us or anything."

Hiroe wasn't sure how to feel. It seemed like she should feel like her privacy had been violated, but the whole thing was just so surreal, she couldn't even muster much outrage. "Does it go everywhere with you?"

"No, Bruno's more of a homebody. But I asked it to come with me to this. I wasn't sure why but I had a feeling its skills might come in handy." He shrugged. "And hey, I was right!"

"How long have you had it?"

"You mean how long have we been friends? Since I was a little kid. I came across it one day while I was out on a swim and when I touched it, realized it could communicate with me. So I'd come visit it every chance I got and we got to be good friends. When I had to leave home—the waters where my family lived were becoming uninhabitable, with fish and plants dying off, so they sent me to college on land—I asked Bruno to come with me. We've been roommates ever since."

"So it's like a pet, right?"

Louvin looked indignant. "Absolutely not! Bruno's more intelligent than anyone I've ever met, and more perceptive too. It actually helps me with my poetry—even though it doesn't have feelings the same exact way we do, it's got an amazing grasp of aquean struggles and what that all means to us. And it's got a great sense of humor. Dude's just fun to hang out with more than anything."

Hiroe had to laugh, strangely charmed despite her best efforts not to be. Even more so when Louvin's eyes lit up at her laughter. It broke the awkward tension that had developed between them.

Without warning, he pulled her into a room they were passing. He pushed her against the wall and kissed her, running his hand up her back under her top. Hiroe's sudden intake of breath seemed to embolden him even more.

Hiroe, despite her best judgment, found herself holding his waist and pulling him to her. She put her hands under his shirt. She couldn't get over his skin, which was a little less damp than before but still felt slippery under her fingers. The way it warmed under her touch was intoxicating.

"What do you think?" he breathed into her ear. "You want to finish what we started?" He pressed against her and she was sorely tempted, both by her arousal and sheer curiosity. But she summoned an ounce of professionalism and pushed him away.

"Maybe later," she said reluctantly.

Louvin looked crestfallen but smiled to hide it and kissed her again, lightly and teasingly. "Let's solve this mystery so later comes soon," he murmured, and she laughed.

"We should go," she said, straightening her top, and led the way out of the room.

They reached an elevator with four numbered buttons. Louvin pushed the fourth, and the car took them up silently. They faced each other in the small compartment. Louvin's eyes never left hers during the brief journey. She thought she saw a smile playing around the edges of his mouth.

The elevator stopped and opened. They were in a small plain area that couldn't even be called a hall or a room. It was a small white box. It looked like a dead end.

"This is where Bruno said she'd be," Louvin said.

Hiroe remembered the doors in the small building on land where she'd prepared to enter Faith's underwater empire. She ran her hands over the plain white wall opposite the elevator, tapping wherever she thought she felt any small irregularity. Eventually the seemingly solid wall parted.

Right inside was another heavy-looking door that looked like it was made of wood, but it glided easily open with a touch.

They stood on the threshold, taking in what they could see of the interior of the room. It was enormous, with large green plants, almost like small trees, blocking most of their view. Hiroe realized she hadn't seen non-aquatic plant life since she'd arrived at the estate.

Louvin cocked his head in the direction of a gap between two of the plants and Hiroe nodded. The room was so dark they couldn't see anything beyond the greenery, but they walked forward as quietly as possible.

They were in a massive bed chamber. The floor looked convincingly like polished marble, though it was probably an illusion like many other surfaces in the home. The walls were hung with gigantic woven tapestries depicting fantastic ocean scenes of aquean men, women, and children swimming among coral reefs and schools of vividly colored fish.

At the other end of the room, a huge canopy bed stood on a raised dais. Hiroe thought she saw a slight figure in the bed, barely a lump under the covers, dwarfed by the outsize scale of the bed itself. Hiroe lifted her hand to Louvin, wordlessly asking him to stay where he was, and walked up to the platform.

As she got near, the first thing she noticed was how the air changed. She couldn't place the smell, but it was all around her and made her think of illness, though it wasn't body odor, or urine, or any of the usual odors associated with a sick bed. Maybe it was an ocean smell somehow permeating the walls. It had a hint of salt, almost of fishiness. Hiroe kept sniffing the air curiously. It wasn't completely unpleasant but it was ... off somehow. She couldn't find another way to categorize her impression of it.

There was no reason for the master bedroom of a lavish mansion to smell like this when every other area Hiroe had been in had either no discernible scent or a pleasant aroma in the air.

Whatever the reason was, she couldn't just keep edging silently up to the bed, especially if that small shape under the blankets was the rich and powerful owner of this estate and hostess of the lavish fundraiser going on downstairs. Hiroe spoke so softly at first that it was nearly a whisper. "Mrs. Benedict?"

No answer. The indistinct shrouded shape didn't move. Hiroe took another step. The odor seemed to double in intensity, and now it was distinctly off-putting, with a mildewy undertone. She thought she could hear soft, labored snoring now. "Mrs. Benedict, is that you?" Louder this time.

She thought she saw a stirring, so she tried again. "Faith, are you all right?"

Now the blankets definitely shifted, making a faint rustling noise. Hiroe thought she could see a face turn to her in the gloom, but it was hard to tell. The figure made a muffled noise, the voice fogged with sleep. Hiroe couldn't make out any words.

She stepped closer still. Seeing a circular pad on the wall next to her, just barely visible, Hiroe took a chance and touched it.

The part of the room she was standing in, including the bed and dais, were suddenly flooded with illumination. Hiroe blinked, her eyes shocked by it. The bed's occupant cried out and a second later, when Hiroe's vision had adjusted enough to see clearly, so did she.

CHAPTER FOURTEEN

The distinctive silver hair clearly identified her. Without it, Hiroe would never have known.

Every part of what would've been the woman's exposed skin—face, neck, and the hand weakly raised as if to defend herself from the light or her intruder—was thickly coated with something mottled and strangely textured.

The coating was colorful, but the colors weren't vibrant like the tapestries around them—some had a sickly muddy tinge, others were bright in the way a poisonous creature broadcasts its deadly nature to the world around it.

"Whoo arr oo?" Faith—or the thing with Faith's hair—slurred. Hiroe's stomach lurched as the thought occurred to her that it sounded like the inside of the woman's mouth was similarly furred with the unknown substance.

Hiroe stepped away instinctively. She looked back to where Louvin was obediently standing where she'd gestured for him to stay, and her stricken face brought him over in a hurry.

He stopped short before he reached Hiroe, his eyes locked on the figure in the bed, now struggling to sit up. "Fuck," he breathed. His face drained of color, turning a sickly whitish green.

"Is that—" Hiroe couldn't accept the thought that was dawning on her.

Just then the Faith-thing let out a terrible muffled shout. She pressed something that was strapped to her hand with a labored movement of her disfigured finger. Hiroe heard a quiet series of beeps and saw a small blue light flash on the device.

"Let's go!" Louvin said. He grabbed Hiroe's arm with uncharacteristic roughness and half-dragged her back through the plants, out of the room, and into the small lobby. He tapped the wall by the elevator several times to call it. "She set off some kind of alarm—we have to get out of here."

He spotted a barely detectable hairline crack in the wall next to the elevator and ran his hand frantically over the area until a door opened, revealing stairs. They heard the nearly silent whoosh of the elevator as it neared their floor, but Louvin pulled Hiroe into the stairwell and tapped at the wall beside the door until it whisked closed, leaving them in near total darkness.

Louvin fumbled around and a yellow glow lit up the darkness. Hiroe realized he'd opened his bag; Bruno was now iridescent. In the strange illumination, she saw Louvin put his finger to his lips as they heard voices out in the hall. Then he started downstairs, moving carefully and making as little sound as possible.

Hiroe followed him gingerly, depending on Bruno's luminescence to keep from tripping.

They reached the bottom, and Louvin found the switch to open the stairwell door. They walked briskly until they found a deserted room. Hiroe saw that he was shaking and still pale.

She had to put words to her own fear. "Was that—aquamycosis?" Hiroe breathed. Louvin nodded. Moisture beaded his upper lip and he scrubbed his face with his hand.

"You don't think you could've been exposed, right?" she said. "You didn't get close to her and she didn't touch—"

"I don't know," he said. "I don't think so, but I don't know." He shook his head. "Unless there's a sporing, which I didn't see, I should be fine. But aqueans have contracted it when there were spores still in the air from a previous one ..." his eyes were wide with fear. "She was so far gone. Aquamycosis gets more communicable the more it takes over."

Hiroe sat, her head spinning. "But she's—"

"Human." Louvin finished her thought. "I know."

"And that's never happened, right?"

"Not that anyone has ever reported." He sighed heavily, looking worriedly at her. It took her a second longer to get to what he must be thinking about.

"Does that mean—I could've caught it in there too?" It was Hiroe's turn to feel sick at the indelible image of Faith Benedict's diseased face and hands.

Louvin spread his hands in a gesture of bewilderment. He looked lost, his face even younger, almost childlike.

"Okay," Hiroe said, faking a sense of control she didn't feel. She stood up, squared her shoulders. "Let's stay calm. We're in the same place as the world's top doctors and scientists when it comes to aquamycosis. We have to talk to some of them, get more information. We can figure this out." His face was breaking her heart. She held out her hand. "We can. We will."

He took her hand and she drew him to her. His lean, suddenly boyish-seeming body collapsed against her and she stumbled a little under the weight, but she held on to him in a tight embrace.

He clung to her too, his face buried in her neck. He wasn't crying exactly, but his breath sounded ragged and she could feel his heart pounding against her. She stroked his back and squeezed him, rocking slightly.

His breathing deepened and slowed. "Thank you," he said into her neck. His lips pressed against her skin, and then suddenly he moved and was kissing her lips fiercely, holding her face in his hands.

His desperate grasp reminded her of how she'd felt in the water, relying on his breath to keep her alive. She tried to hold him the way he'd held her throughout that ordeal, calm and purposeful in the face of an uncertain fate.

She imagined her kisses were giving him back the air he'd loaned her, even though she felt like they might both be drowning.

CHAPTER FIFTEEN

When he was calmer, they made their way
back to the main area of the home. The
attendees had moved to the cocktail reception
where a new dizzying array of food and drink
awaited them.

Hiroe and Louvin slipped in unnoticed and
joined the crowd. They made their way to
Demonte by way of the bar, both drinking their
cocktails faster than they ordinarily would.

When they got to him, Hiroe handed him
his favorite drink, a tumbler of neat cognac,
and he thanked her with a tight smile.

He was disbelieving of their story at first, but had no choice but to accept it. He in turn had noticed more people missing, though the numbers of newly disappeared had slowed to a trickle. Three more guests had vanished by the time he'd made it back to the auditorium for the end of the final keynote speech.

They were deciding which scientist to talk to first when they noticed a change of mood in the room. Something was attracting the attention of the assembled guests. Small groups of them in increasing numbers began to murmur and point.

Outside the floor-to-ceiling windows, among the waving seaweed, colorful coral, and picturesque fish, a number of figures could be seen indistinctly, swimming toward the building. It was eerie but mesmerizing watching them approach.

"Is this part of the show?" someone said in a low voice, mirroring what Demonte had said earlier when Lottie's voice had taken over the program. The words carried clearly through the hush that had fallen over the partygoers.

"Wow," Louvin breathed.

"What is it?" Hiroe whispered to him. He didn't seem to hear her, his eyes fixed on the spectacle outside.

The swimming figures came into focus as they got closer. They were aquean, at least two dozen, maybe more. Male and female, old and young, all wearing black with understated iridescent patterns that only became visible when they were very close, they swam in a sort of loose formation until they were lined up outside the windows, looking straight inside. Hiroe found herself shifting uncomfortably, though she was fairly sure it was one-way glass and they couldn't see inside.

After a minute or two of staying in one place, perfectly still, the aqueans floated closer to the windows, their arms making sweeping movements.

As they gestured, they opened their hands. Seemingly pouring from their palms, small dots of light, beads of luminescent material, perhaps, or small sea creatures, swirled around in captivating patterns before resolving into lines and curves that became letters, which became words, which formed a sentence.

"STOP EXPLOITING US," the lights read. Then they scrambled and became other letters, other words. "THIS IS STOLEN WATER." Sentences appeared one by one. "YOU'RE PARTICIPATING IN GENOCIDE."

Hiroe tore her gaze from the spectacle long enough to look at Louvin. He was glued to what was going on outside, eyes shining with tears. He slowly raised a fist until he was holding it high above his head. Hiroe doubted the swimmers could see him. She was pretty sure he knew that too.

Something else behind Louvin caught Hiroe's eye. About twenty feet away, someone was watching Louvin intently, speaking low into a device on his finger. The guard they'd decided was not a guard. His eyes flicked to the demonstrators outside the window, then back to Louvin. Hiroe quietly tried to get the poet's attention, but he was raptly focused.

The onlookers inside gave a collective gasp, and Hiroe turned back to the windows. Behind the protesters, a handful of human divers with masks appeared through the water. No sound made it into the room, but the intent of the divers was clear—to break up the demonstration.

The aqueans resisted, moving away from the divers, slipping out of their grasp several times. But more divers came, and more humans in aquatic vehicles, and the demonstrators were soon outnumbered and surrounded on all sides. Hiroe's stomach churned as she watched them lock arms and start singing a song. She couldn't hear it, but what was happening was perfectly, poignantly clear.

"What are you doing?" Hiroe heard Louvin say behind her, and it snapped her out of her hypnotic state.

The not-guard reached Louvin just as she turned around. The man was about the same height as Louvin, maybe even a touch shorter, but he probably outweighed him by fifty pounds or more. Hiroe watched in shock as he grabbed Louvin, pinned his arms behind him, and touched his wrists with a device that imprisoned them in cuffs.

"What's going on?" Hiroe demanded. "Who are you?" The man didn't answer or even look at her.

Demonte spoke up. "This man did nothing wrong. You have no right to detain him."

The not-guard looked at them, unimpressed, and answered at last. "Actually I do. I'm FBI, and it's within my power to detain someone if I have reasonable suspicion of a crime. And I have reasonable suspicion that this young man has been involved in the planning and execution of the activity outside, which is trespassing and unlawful assembly."

Hiroe glanced back at the window. The protesters were being detained and taken away, some submitting with calm resignation, others struggling ferociously against their captors, their mouths stretched in screams that Hiroe couldn't hear.

In the brief moment her head had been turned, the agent started dragging Louvin away. "Wait!" Hiroe cried, following him. "Where are you taking him?"

"You don't have to worry, ma'am; he'll be given a chance to explain himself."

"But where are you going? Where's your identification? Can he have a lawyer?"

He implacably ignored her, and when she followed him to the door of the room, another man stepped between them, restraining her temporarily while Louvin and his captor disappeared from sight.

CHAPTER SIXTEEN

Hiroe felt sick. It was clear the man wasn't going to leave the doorway anytime soon, so she retreated into the room.

The whole evening she'd passed through the crowd unnoticed, managing to stay unobtrusive and blend into the surroundings. Now she saw countless curious eyes and heard furtive whispers. Some looked concerned or sympathetic, but most of them seemed to regard this as just another form of entertainment. Her face burned. She hated this kind of attention.

Her mind was racing. Was the FBI here at Faith's request or had they come without her knowledge? Were they here specifically to thwart a possible protest or did they just happen to be in the right place at the right time?

Faith. She'd momentarily forgotten what she'd seen on the fourth floor. Now Louvin wouldn't be able to help explore the mystery of a human contracting aquamycosis or get advice on his potential exposure. She wasn't sure how to try and locate Louvin or get him legal help, and she didn't see how she could do that *and* try to find out more about what was going on.

She lurched back to Demonte. She felt lost, and her former mentor was the closest thing to home. She bit her lip, trying to choke back tears and collect herself before she returned to his side. She didn't want Demonte to see it. But he was watching her closely, and when she got close enough, he reached out and wrapped her in a tight hug.

She couldn't remember the last time that had happened, other than the stiff greetings they occasionally exchanged. After a hesitation she reciprocated. His rough cheek against hers, his solid body, felt real and comforting.

She knew the smell of his cologne and cognac mingling together. They hadn't hugged much even when they were working together, but they'd spent long hours together, sometimes in close quarters, so she'd become accustomed to this scent.

The last time she remembered smelling that combination was when he told her about his plan to leave to start Static. They were alone in a car of a high-speed train, heading back to D.C. from an assignment. She was flush with their success—they'd been covering a high-profile murder for years and they'd just conducted an explosive interview with the convicted killer. It had aired live and the reaction was already massive.

She and Demonte were celebrating with recyclable cups from the train dining car, pouring shots of his favorite cognac and toasting their success. But his face gradually grew serious, and finally she asked him what was going on.

He drained his cup and poured another finger of cognac. He stared at the small container, and didn't look up even when he began speaking.

"Hiroe, this is my last assignment," he said.

She took a second to let it sink in, then found her voice. "Did you get promoted? Are you gonna be a director?" she asked. She felt a tug of loss at the thought of not going out on adventures together, but she was mainly happy for him. Plus, she thought, she wouldn't be far behind him now. If Demonte got promoted, she could probably expect her own promotion or raise soon after.

But he shook his head, still gazing at his cognac, swirling it slightly in the cup. "I'm leaving Global Media."

Through the rest of the conversation, as he told her about Static, she felt as if they were getting farther and farther apart, even though they still sat close together in the small rail car, surrounded by the mingled scents of cologne and cognac.

She managed to say the things she thought someone should say to a co-worker who was leaving for a better opportunity. She didn't say the one thought that loomed over all the others, the question that left her heartbroken, her stomach clenched with hurt and anger.

She waited until she'd said goodbye at the train station and gotten home to her apartment to cry. Then she did, long pitiful sobs. She felt ridiculous, a fortysomething woman wailing like a child. But no one was there to see her except herself.

She'd looked in the mirror in her bathroom when it was over and washed her puffy eyes with cold water, a question circling in her mind, the unspoken question that reared up every time she saw him, that had caused the growing coldness and antagonism between them over the years.

Why didn't you ask me to come with you?

The blow to her personal and professional egos were so intertwined in that one question, she couldn't ever tell which was the bigger betrayal.

Even now, she wondered that: Why? Why hadn't he wanted her to join Static? But his tight embrace made her feel more valued, more acknowledged by him than she had since that day in the rail car. She felt as if the past ten years had never happened and they were back to the way they'd been, but better, because he was holding her in a way he never had before.

"You like that kid a whole lot, huh?" Demonte asked, and she pulled away from him, the spell abruptly broken. Her face felt hot as she tried rolling her eyes, not sure how convincing she was being.

"Come on, Dee," she said, using her old nickname for him and the most dismissive tone she could manage. "You saw what just happened. He was basically profiled—they made an example of him because he's aquean and dared to show solidarity with those protesters."

"Hey, you don't know that," he said, not sounding like he was even convincing himself.

"Maybe he did help organize it. Maybe the FBI has proof."

"That's bullshit," she said. "If they had proof, then they had advance knowledge, and they could have taken him earlier. There was no reason for doing it the way they did—unless they were profiling him." She paused, thinking. "Or looking for some excuse to arrest him in particular."

Her eyebrows furrowed. "I'm worried something's going to happen to him in custody. You know what aqueans are up against. It's the same damn story of what your ancestors faced, Dee, and mine too. Things got gradually better for us, but they've found a new target, a new group that people don't understand and are willing to let be oppressed."

"That's it, now I know you dig the guy," Demonte said with a chuckle. "You've always been cynical, but I've never known you to be a social justice warrior." He saw her face and sobered. "I'm sorry. I was just trying to make you laugh. Or at least get annoyed and tell me off." He shrugged. "I get it, it was hard to see him taken away like that. But what are we supposed to do? Fight the FBI?"

Hiroe exhaled. "I guess I don't know. But given everything that's happened tonight—the weird thing Lottie said on the sound system, the other people disappearing, whatever the fuck is going on with Faith Benedict—I refuse to just accept that this arrest, or detainment or whatever you call it, is on the level.

"Something really odd is going on here. Maybe several things, coincidentally, or maybe it's all connected. But I can't just let them take away the guy who started trying to figure out what's really happening. There's a chance he's been taken for that, or for another equally bad reason, and I can't assume everything's okay for him right now."

This time Demonte didn't try to come up with a jokey reply. He looked serious, as if he were trying to think of a course of action, but his head was shaking slightly. Hiroe felt her heart sink. She stared desolately at the ground, trying to tune out the din of the guests, who had gradually returned to their drinking and chatter as if nothing had happened.

That's when she spotted something that might help them.

She reached down and scooped up Louvin's rucksack. He must've put it on the floor before he raised his fist to support the protesters, and it had lain crumpled there, apparently unnoticed by any of the guests or staff.

"Is that—?" Demonte started to ask and stopped in disbelief.

"Yep," Hiroe said with the first glimmer of hope she'd had since Louvin had been taken away. "Bruno."

CHAPTER SEVENTEEN

"I didn't do anything," Louvin said for the tenth time as he was half-dragged along by two agents. He knew better than to resist, but they seemed to always keep him slightly off balance with unexpected pushes and pulls that made him stumble. Then they'd yank him up roughly as if they thought he'd been trying to fight them.

This time when he said it, the agent stopped and threw him against a wall. His bound wrists banged against it painfully, the plastic restraints cutting into his skin, but he suppressed the urge to recoil from the wall.

"Okay then," the agent said. "You're not here because of the demonstration. So why exactly are you here?"

"Faith Benedict invited me here," Louvin said, trying to sound compliant and reasonable despite his pounding heart. "She said she'd heard of my poetry performances and wanted me to open the program with one. I knew what she's been doing for aquamycosis research, so I said yes. That's it."

"You acted pretty pleased by the demonstrations for someone who's on board with this event," the agent said.

"Because I respect dissenting viewpoints and the right to free speech," Louvin replied, speaking rapidly but trying to sound dispassionate. "Just because I agreed to come here doesn't mean I agree with Faith building her home by the Trench, or with her giving money to anti-science fringe theorists. We don't all have to approach things the same way; I chose to speak at the event, but I think protesting the event is also valid and important."

"So it was just a coincidence, even though you've been at similar demonstrations yourself?"

"Yes. I swear."

"And your sister working here?" the man snapped. "Is that just another coincidence?"

Louvin was puzzled. What did that have to do with the protests? "Yes. At least, I think so. I guess Faith could've heard of me through Villanna …"

The agent pulled him off the wall, swung around and slammed him chest-first against the other one. "Why don't you cut the bullshit and tell me what's really going on? What were you doing sneaking around with the Black guy and the Asian chick earlier?"

Louvin struggled to stay calm and not resist even as the agent pushed his head against the wall, his cheek grinding into the surface. "It's like we told you then, we noticed some people had gone missing. We were worried they might be lost or hurt like that woman who broke her leg, so we were trying to find them. That's all."

The agent grabbed him again and he flinched, but this time he started dragging him down the hall again. Louvin staggered and almost fell but didn't complain.

The two men took Louvin in a water car to a nondescript building that hadn't been on his tour earlier. Once the water drained from the port, they took him past rooms from which he could hear voices, angry and frightened.

His heart ached; he'd recognized several demonstrators from past actions he'd participated in. He was transported in an elevator to a lower floor, and here there were no sounds of any other prisoners.

The agent's assistant tapped the wall to open a door, and Louvin was shoved between the shoulder blades, his hands suddenly freed from the shackles at the same time. He stumbled in, barely keeping himself from falling, and turned around.

The two men stood in the doorway. "Take this time to get your story straight," the agent said. "We're going to figure out what's going on with you, so you'd do well to cooperate with us when we come back."

The door slid shut, and Louvin was alone in the quiet, bland room. It didn't appear to have been built to be a cell; the only furnishing was an air mattress with no bedding.

Louvin sat down on the mattress and put his head between his hands. He retraced the night's events with disbelief. How had it all led to this—locked away alone, suspected of what, he wasn't sure exactly? The agents hadn't spent much time asking him about the protest, so he doubted that was the real reason he'd been detained.

He thought about Faith Benedict. She hadn't gotten a good look at him in her room, had she? Could this be retaliation for discovering her secret? It didn't seem likely. Maybe Bruno could help him find out who the agent was working for if …

Bruno. Louvin's body flooded with panic as he realized for the first time that his bag was gone.

He retraced his steps in his mind, finally concluding that he'd dropped the bag at the party and forgotten to pick it back up.

He pictured the bag being thrown out—compacted into nothing, incinerated, or abandoned somewhere. His anguish overcame him and he collapsed across the bed. The thought of losing his best friend outweighed even his fear that he could've caught aquamycosis from Faith.

Still, he knew Bruno was practically immortal. He was heartbroken and wracked with guilt, but he took some comfort knowing he'd survive whatever happened, and maybe they could find one another again. Hiroe, on the other hand … he could only hope she was finding help for her possible exposure to aquamycosis.

Despite his worry, thinking about her made him remember their furtive encounters, and his heart raced. She'd been immediately striking to him, from the moment he saw her. He'd never had a serious attraction to a human before, but there was something about her. He was a little scared of how she made him feel, since he was pretty sure she was just having fun with him.

That thought made him feel even more alone. He slumped lower, overwhelmed and hopeless.

CHAPTER EIGHTEEN

"How do you know this'll even work with a human?" Demonte asked. "Or whether it really happened at all before—maybe the kid already knew where Faith Benedict was."

Hiroe had thought of both possibilities. She had to at least give it a try.

They'd slipped unobtrusively out of the party—the goon at the door had left by then and they were free to exit the ballroom—and found a secluded spot. Hiroe had set the bag down and unfastened its closures. There was the yellowish mass, not appearing to move or react when exposed to the light.

She grimaced with slight disgust but tried to regulate her reaction before touching it. Who was she to deny the existence or—well, not humanity exactly—her mind lost its way on that particular train of thought. She steeled herself, tried to think positive thoughts, and lowered her hand slowly onto the blob.

She'd expected a wet, slippery, viscous thing. None of those words described what she was feeling. It wasn't like air, liquid, or solid. It wasn't cold or warm. It wasn't wet or dry. It wasn't pleasant or unpleasant. It wasn't like anything she'd ever touched before.

What it *was* was sentient. As soon as she came into contact with it, she felt its acknowledgment and awareness of her. It knew who she was. It didn't say her name—didn't speak in words inside her mind or anything—but she knew it knew. The power of that feeling pushed the physical sensation of touching it out of her mind.

She shut her eyes and Bruno came into full focus in her mind. She felt its worry about Louvin and its gladness about her getting in contact with it. She understood that it didn't have those emotions at all, but that its awareness had some analog to the emotions she was experiencing. It didn't care in the way that a person cared, but it was deeply involved in Louvin's life.

It managed to share with her in a few sensations, a few weirdly colorful images, the long history it had with Louvin, starting with the boy swimming innocently over the ocean floor as Bruno, also much smaller then, sat in the sand, equally innocent of the fact that it was about to meet a person who would become its closest companion.

Hiroe saw in a flood all the times the two had lain together at the bottom of the ocean, sharing Louvin's hopes and fears for his future, Bruno's quiet observation of life. Then their life together on dry land, Bruno experiencing Louvin's every triumph and failure with him and providing a feeling of home in the midst of the alien world he'd been dropped into.

In a very short time, Hiroe believed Bruno: It had some equivalent to friendship with

Louvin and some sort of drive to help him that was as strong in its own way as Hiroe's.

She sensed, too, that it knew what she and Louvin had done, but rather than feel embarrassed, she felt more comfortable. To Bruno, their acts were as elemental as the tide, or its own self-contained reproductive method. It imparted to her some understanding of how that worked and how it felt to Bruno as well, and she took it as Bruno's attempt to share something equally intimate so she wouldn't feel they an imbalance in terms of what they knew about one another.

She pushed her wanting to help Louvin into the mass, and they communed on the problem. Though no complete solution presented itself, they agreed that finding him was the first priority. Bruno shared her viewpoint that he might be in danger in the hands of the agents.

Bruno then stretched its awareness. She almost felt it envelop her and then expand beyond her. She saw things it passed almost like they were on a heat map, except it wasn't temperature that made them colorful. It was her human mind's interpretation of Bruno's version of vision that it was sharing with her.

It spread into the ocean and past the buildings Hiroe already knew about. Past that, another building stood. Less adorned than the others, at least as far as Hiroe could tell through the distorted filter of Bruno's sight, and without the elaborate gardens around it. She couldn't see any tunnels to it and wondered, heart sinking, if it could only be reached by car.

Bruno went inside, spreading through the walls as easily as it had the ocean waters. They came across occupants. Hiroe understood through Bruno's understanding that these were aqueans, housed three or four to a small room, seated on the floor, lying down, pacing the few scant feet they could in the cramped space.

Aqueans, but not Louvin. Bruno confirmed this in each room it expanded into. These must be the protesters, they agreed. It was spreading more slowly—it was getting to its limit, and it took longer to sense the intricacies of people rather than ocean topography or building layouts. They encountered two humans as well, one walking the halls, another seated in a chair. Guards, Hiroe and Bruno concurred.

Then it found a lower floor, a basement carved into the ocean bed. It spread downward and there he was, a lone figure, slouching on the floor, his back to the wall. Hiroe's relief and whatever Bruno would call what it experienced dovetailed and she felt as if she might pass out from the combined emotion.

A sensation of vertigo came over her as Bruno's shared vision receded at lightning speed, returning their awareness to the building they were in, then the room, then the small space the two of them occupied together, and the next thing Hiroe felt was her back pressing into the floor, and Demonte's hand tapping her cheek, coaxing her to wake up. She'd fallen when she lost consciousness, her hand slipping out of the bag and losing contact with Bruno.

When she was lucid enough to speak, she told Demonte what Bruno had shown her.

"So he's here, he's alive, and he's unhurt," Demonte said. "Those are three good things we didn't know before. Could Bruno tell what he was thinking?"

Hiroe shook her head. "It can only really read minds through touching someone," she said. "If it's in a room with someone it can get a pretty good sense of what's going on, like reading their energy or body chemistry or something. But as far away as Louvin was, it couldn't sense anything about his mood or thoughts. Judging from the way he was sitting he didn't look seriously injured, but we don't know whether or not he was in pain."

"Did you see any guards?"

"Only two," Hiroe replied. "Unless we didn't get through the whole building before Bruno got tired out."

Demonte shook his head. "It's too fucking weird that you talk about that goo like it's a person."

Hiroe cringed inwardly, thinking of Bruno picking up on their conversation, but also not wanting to get into it with Demonte. "It's

definitely not a person, but it's very …
compatible with us. It's easy to be with. I can
see why Louvin is friends with it."

She could see Demonte's skepticism, but he
changed the subject. "So what now?"

"Well." Hiroe set her jaw stubbornly. "I
want to get him out."

"You're kidding," Demonte said flatly.

She bit her lip. "He—he didn't do this. And
if he did, how is it a federal crime to protest, or
organize a protest? Whether or not he was
involved, he was not trespassing; Faith invited
him here!" She took a shaky breath. "Bruno's
worried too. It doesn't think the FBI guy was
being above board about why he took Louvin
away."

Demonte sighed with an air of resignation.
"Okay," he said. "Say you're right—how do
you plan to do it?"

"I—I can't," Hiroe said, her voice low with
shame. "There's no tunnel, so the only way to
get there is through the water. I know I
couldn't do it alone, and plus I'd be no use

once I was out in it. I'd freeze. I'd panic." She looked steadily at him.

"Oh you're fucking kidding me," he said. He knew she wasn't. "You expect me to risk my whole career? My life? For some punk kid you have a crush on?"

"Dee, please," she said, with effort. "You have to get him out of there."

He sighed again, running his hand over his close-cropped, graying curls and then scrubbing at his stubbled cheek.

"Damn," he said. "I forgot what a pain in the ass you were to work with."

CHAPTER NINETEEN

She described the way to the prison as best she could, but insisted he take Bruno with him in case he got lost.

She touched the blob with some affection to tell it to take care of Demonte, that he really was a good guy despite his bluster.

Bruno understood. It didn't have any need for acceptance from humans anyway. She asked it for a favor before they left, and despite being a little worn out from its previous seeking, it obliged.

A few minutes later, she parted ways with Demonte and Bruno, and headed purposefully in the direction Bruno had just shown her.

* * *

Demonte was also following Bruno's directions, albeit secondhand. And that was the way he wanted it to stay. He'd be goddamned if he was going to stick his hand in a bag full of slime. It was bad enough he was about to go try to outsmart the FBI just to please a woman who didn't give two shits about him.

And who must give a lot more than that about the kid, if she'd willingly entered a water car with him. He'd never seen her so much as take a river cruise, or go for a day at the beach, as long as he'd known her. Any body of water made her tense up, even start shaking if she got close enough to it.

She'd told him what happened with Elise, once, while they'd been drinking heavily after work together, and she'd begged him not to bring it up later.

He never did, but he thought about it every time he saw her fear around water, and he tried to shield her from any assignments that might put her in a triggering situation. He was surprised she was holding it together as well as she had, being deep underwater for an extended period of time. Maybe she'd grown out of it somewhat, or maybe not having him to protect her had forced her to find an inner strength she—and he—didn't even know she'd had.

He tried to push the old days out of his head. It'd been a while since he'd talked his way into a place he wasn't meant to be under false pretenses, and he needed to get in the right frame of mind for it.

He found his way to a water car port that looked like it could be the closest to where he needed to go. He picked a vehicle and dumped the bag of Bruno in the passenger seat, then used the touch screen to dial security. He could tell by the voice that the man who answered was aquean, and he smoothly shifted his own vocal inflections to match when he spoke.

"Hi," he said. "I gotta take a guest to their quarters and the car isn't recognizing my print because I messed up my damn thumb earlier today." He laughed ruefully. "I'll get a new ID tomorrow, but could you give me a guest code to get me through the night?"

He lowered his voice. "And if you'd find it in your heart to not tell anyone, I'd appreciate it. It wasn't my fault I cut my thumb, but you know how they can be."

His fellow aquean did indeed know how they could be and was more than happy to give him a guest code and keep his secret.

He entered the code and started the car. Since he didn't know what the prison building was called, he steered the vehicle himself using the touch screen. Once he got the hang of it, he enjoyed driving. It wasn't something anyone got to do much of anymore.

The beautiful gardens and exotic fish gave way to a plainer, less scenic landscape, but the benefit was that his view was unobstructed; he soon spotted the building. He'd figured there wouldn't be an unobtrusive way to approach it, and he was right. So he steered directly toward the port at the front, entered the dock, and watched the water drain out around him.

He was tempted to leave Louvin's rucksack behind; its coarse fabric and worn appearance didn't match the role he was about to play. But he didn't want to catch heat from Hiroe or her boy toy about their pal the blob, so he'd just have to make it work. He slung the bag over his shoulder and left the vehicle.

The main door to the building was unlocked, but it led only to a small foyer with a locked glass door. Demonte tapped a button he assumed would call someone, and a minute or two later, a confused-looking human guard came into view behind the glass. His voice came clearly through the door. "What can I do for you?"

Demonte adopted a frazzled tone. "You can maybe build a time machine and go back to the past and pick me up from the main house half an hour ago!"

The confused frown on the other man's face deepened. "What?"

Demonte groaned. "Look, never mind. It was a joke. Clearly no one got the memo that I was coming to meet my new client, Louvin Interre, but I'm here now so it's water under the bridge. No pun intended. Could you just let me in so I can see him?"

"Well, I don't think—" the guard started, but Demonte interrupted in a harassing, condescending tone.

"I know, I *know* you don't think, and that's not what you're paid for. But what *I'm* paid for, and very well at that, is coming to the aid of my clients. Interre must have generous friends up top to be able to afford my rush rate, so I'd rather not keep him waiting."

The guard hesitated a little longer, and Demonte started to feel inward despair, but he channeled it into how his character was feeling about letting down his client.

"What's going on? Is my client in solitary? Did he do something more serious than I've heard about or are you just tormenting him for no reason? Are you trying to bar him from due process? Has he been harmed? If so, things are about to get—very public for you here."

"No!" the guard said, alarmed. "He's not—I mean, he's in a room alone, but it's not solitary. He's fine—no injuries at all. And he's just in there for that protest, far as I know. But I'm not sure if I can let anyone in, even lawyers. I should contact Agent Brooks."

"I see," Demonte started to downshift his tone to a friendlier, confiding one. "I get it. You don't want to do anything that's not spelled out. It's a weird situation you've got here, with this ad hoc prison, right?"

"Right," the guard said, sounding relieved.

"I understand your dilemma, I really do. That's why I want you to try and understand mine, okay? If I can't assure my clients—who seem extremely invested in this young man— very *very* soon that he's unhurt, they are going to leverage their considerable influence to unleash a—I believe the legal term is complete motherfucking shitstorm to the media. You get me? Much as I'd like to take your word for it, I cannot deceive my clients when they ask if I've seen Interre and if he's okay. And I cannot wait around for a fucking bureaucrat to wrap me up in a bunch of red tape. Believe me, *you* can't afford the delay either."

The guard looked distraught. "Give me a second, sir, okay?" He disappeared from the window and Demonte waited, his suit soaked through under his arms. He braced himself for a team of armed guards to burst through the door and arrest him. Or worse, for Brooks (who he assumed must be the man who had detained Louvin) to arrive at the prison in a water car and recognize him from the party.

Instead, the guard returned with one other, slightly older and more suspicious-looking man. He questioned Demonte, who explained it all again and tried to maintain his power-lawyer alter ego convincingly. He was utterly shocked, however, when it worked. The guards opened the door and let him in. The first guard led him to an elevator and down to the basement.

A door was unlocked with a few swift taps and slid soundlessly open. Louvin raised his head at the change in light and his eyes widened with surprise. Demonte shook his head slightly, praying the punk kid saw it and understood not to blow his cover, and resumed his fast talk.

"Mr. Interre, I'm relieved to see you unhurt. I was starting to have my doubts when they wouldn't let me see you." He turned to the guard. "Congratulations! You've just saved yourself and your whole outfit some embarrassing and unnecessary press. Now I need to see my client alone, please."

"But—" the guard stammered. Demonte rolled his eyes and let out an exaggerated sigh.

"Here we go again. Since we already know how this ended last time, can we skip the part where I threaten you with my powerful clients and their money and status, and get to the part where you allow this young man to see his lawyer in private? He is, from what I understand, being detained on nonviolent and—let's be honest—fairly innocuous charges. So I fail to understand this treatment."

The guard began backing out halfway through his speech and was standing just outside the cell by the end of it. "I'll give you, um, ten minutes, and then I'm coming back down," he said, sounding cowed.

Demonte spread his hands. "That's all I ever wanted, my friend," he said. The guard didn't waste any time going back down the hallway toward the elevator.

As soon as he was out of sight, Demonte turned back toward Louvin.

"Okay, kid," he said. "There has got to be electronic surveillance here, because that brilliant specimen appears to be second in command in an army of two, and I find it hard to believe they're really the only ones responsible for all these prisoners. I imagine if anyone sees what just happened, they're going to come in a hurry. I'd say we have five minutes tops to bust you out of here. Any bright ideas? Because I don't like any of the ideas I've got, which all involve assaulting and imprisoning federal officers."

Louvin had been speechless the whole time, and now he shook his head, dazed with the sudden turn of events. But then his eyes fell on his old rucksack. They lit up with surprised joy, and then something dawned on him.

"I need to talk to Bruno," he told Demonte. "I need to see if it's up for something pretty taxing." He set his jaw determinedly. "Also? I'm not leaving here without helping the protesters."

CHAPTER TWENTY

Demonte emerged from the elevator. The guard was standing by it, waiting. "Did you lock the cell door?" he asked.

Demonte looked scornful. "Of course I did, and that should be something you can check from here, isn't it?" The guard nodded and tapped a wrist device. He stared at it and his face brightened with relief. "Can I see you out, sir?" he said hopefully.

"In a minute," Demonte said. "Where's your colleague? I need to talk to you both about my client's treatment."

"In the office, probably," the guard said, sounding slightly despondent that he hadn't gotten rid of Demonte as quickly as he'd hoped to. But he perked up with new resolve. "Let's go there on your way out." He was brisk and confident now, the end of this confusing incident hopefully in sight. He didn't seem to notice that the previously bulging bag on Demonte's shoulder was now sagging and empty-looking.

In the office, Demonte laid out a string of demands to the two men, making them up as he went along, reasonable requests mixed with a few outlandish ones. The head guard tapped notes into a device and murmured about how they'd check with their superiors to see what they could do. They kept agreeing to try to fulfill all of his demands, saying anything to get rid of him peacefully, until he abruptly stood.

"Well, gentlemen, I'm cautiously optimistic that you'll treat my client well until we can prove he's innocent of these trumped-up charges. I thank you for your time, and your service to our country." He hoped the flourish wasn't too over the top, but both of the men flashed relieved grins and led him to the entrance.

He held the door of the dock open a little longer, finding a few more things to tell them. Then he stood by the open door of his vehicle, fidgeting with his suit and taking his time placing the bag in the car. The guards were watching, he was sure. He finally got into the car and took off.

Next to him in the apparently empty passenger seat, Louvin's rough-cut hair appeared, hovering in the air like the Cheshire cat's smile. The rest of him slowly came into view, as did the transparent coating on him, which slowly returned to its bright yellow hue as it slid down and began to resume its place in the bag. Demonte was repulsed and fascinated and impressed, but he assumed an air of nonchalance.

"Couldn't you keep your blob suit on a little longer?" he asked. "You're gonna have to keep a low profile now that you're an escaped criminal, and that'd be an easy way, if you just stayed invisible."

Louvin shook his head. "Bruno tires quickly when it does something like that. It would've fallen off me soon anyway from sheer exhaustion. It needs time to recharge now."

Demonte shrugged. "What about the other prisoners? Did you—?"

"Unlocked their doors, left them open a crack," Louvin said. "I left it up to them if they want to make a break for it or stay and take their chances with the justice system."

"How'd you get the doors unlocked?" Demonte asked, his curiosity showing despite himself.

"Bruno," Louvin said, smiling affectionately at the slimy mass as it slowly made its way back into the rucksack. "It was coating my fingers, so it figured out the order of the taps that entered the codes earlier."

By now they were at the other dock, and Demonte steered their car into its spot, amazed there hadn't been any sign of guards or security staff. "Let's find Hiroe," he said.

CHAPTER TWENTY-ONE

Hiroe traced the mental map Bruno had left inside her, down hallways and through tunnels, hurrying so the target it had identified hopefully wouldn't move too far away from the spot before she got there.

She turned a corner and spotted her. "Villanna!" she called. Louvin's sister turned and smiled when she saw her.

"Hiroe, right?" She walked back the way she'd come, her crisp white uniform setting off her beautiful light aqua skin. She hugged Hiroe, who marveled again at the girl's delicate frame. "How's my pesky big brother? Off making more trouble, chasing crazy theories?"

"Yeah, pretty much." Hiroe felt guilty withholding the truth, but hopefully Demonte would rescue him and it wouldn't matter. She couldn't afford to have Villanna completely distracted and Hiroe's purpose for talking to her derailed. This was important to Louvin too, she told herself to assuage her guilt.

Instead she told Villanna about what she and Louvin had seen in Faith Benedict's bedroom. Villanna's eyes got wider as she listened, but she didn't question Hiroe's account. Her lip quivered and she blinked away tears. Hiroe felt sympathy but stayed carefully neutral.

"So what I'm wondering, Villanna, is why you told me and Louvin that Faith was fine." The girl tried to say something, but her voice shook, and she began crying uncontrollably.

"I was lying," she said between ragged sobs. Hiroe waited as she took deep breaths and sniffled, slowly calming down. "We all just wanted her to get through the fundraiser before going public about it. We didn't want a mass panic, or for Faith's sickness to distract from the cause.

"She'd been doing okay until recently. Then her symptoms flared up worse than we've ever seen them on anyone. That's when we decided we needed to organize this event. We could raise money, raise awareness, and maybe some of the doctors and scientists who'd been working independently could reach breakthroughs in their thinking if we just got them in the same place for a couple days."

Her eyes shone with more than tears. "It means the world to her, even more so now that she's ... sick herself. We were completely careful to quarantine her and everyone in direct contact with her from the guests." Her eyes narrowed. "At least until you two went looking for her ..."

"But I don't understand how a human caught it," Hiroe said. "It's never jumped species that you know of, right?"

Villanna shook her head. "No, this is the first time. But it's the same disease. It acts about the same way as it does in aqueans too."

"She looked pretty good in the holographs earlier tonight," Hiroe said. "How long ago were they filmed?"

"They weren't really her," Villanna said. "Not exactly anyway. They used existing holographic data of her and programmed it with what we needed her to say for the event."

"How long has she had it, that you know of?"

"About six months," Villanna said, lower lip quivering. "It was beyond horrible when we found out, but it made everyone even more determined. We haven't quite developed a cure yet, but one of our scientists discovered something that suppresses symptoms almost entirely. It was amazing; she went back to normal, practically."

"So what happened?" Hiroe asked.

Villanna sniffled again. "We don't know," she said. "Maybe her body got acclimated to the drug? Maybe her aquamycosis is entering a stage we haven't seen yet and don't fully understand. Faith has lived much longer—about three times as long—than any aquean we know of who has caught aquamycosis and not recovered on their own. We think it's the symptom-blocking medicine that kept her going, but it could also have something to do with the way the disease interacts with a human's immune system. There's a lot we don't know about it at this point."

"Including whether it's transmittable from her back to an aquean?" Hiroe said with dread.

Villanna looked as if she were going to burst into tears again. "Yes, that's one thing we do know. Inesse, one of our aides, was infected early on, before we had the symptoms suppressed. There was a sporing and her hazard suit wasn't totally sealed, and—" Villanna shook her head sadly.

"There wasn't a sporing while we were in there," Hiroe said with hope. "Does that mean—"

"Not necessarily," Villanna said with reluctance. "You have better odds, of course, but if there was one recently, if there were any lingering in the air ..."

Hiroe's stomach lurched. "You said ... you think you're close to a cure?"

Villanna nodded, unsmiling. "It might be a few months though." She brightened. "But, if you or Louvin were infected, I could make sure you had enough of the symptom suppressant to hold aquamycosis at bay, hopefully until we find a cure!" She beckoned. "Come with me!"

She led Hiroe to a cold storage room, ducked inside, and emerged with something small in her hand.

"Here," she said. "This will keep you free of symptoms for about a month. If you start showing signs of aquamycosis after that, I'll make sure you both get extra doses."

She held out her hand; two tiny vials, each with a small rubber-capped needle, lay in her palm. "I think you should take one now. It's completely harmless if you don't have the disease; no side effects at all. You can take the other one to Louvin."

Hiroe took one and pulled the protective bead from the needle tip. "Where do I inject it?" she asked.

"It doesn't matter," Villanna said. "It's foolproof. Do you want me to do it for you?" Hiroe shook her head. She held up her forearm and steeled herself, then drove the needle in.

She barely felt anything. The vial emptied and she felt immediately better, safer.

"Thank you again," she said. "Apparently you saving my life is going to be our little thing, huh?"

Villanna managed a laugh. "Glad to help," she said. Before she could say anything else, a notification beeped on her wrist. She looked at it. "I've got to go take care of something," she said. "You'll get this to my brother right away and tell him how important it is to take it, right?"

"I promise I'll do everything I can," Hiroe said.

"Thank you," Villanna said. "I know things seem awful now, but I really do think they'll get better soon. Thank you for being a good friend to my brother, Hiroe."

Hiroe felt her face get warm, but she merely said "you're welcome" and they parted ways.

CHAPTER TWENTY-TWO

Brooks surveyed the party, which, far from winding down, was becoming more raucous and festive as the night wore on, as he spoke low into his ring.

"No updates on the main mission, but we're still investigating," he said. "We detained the demonstrators with no problems." He paused.

"There've been a couple of wrinkles. One of the top medical staff, Villanna Interre? Her brother's on the speaker list. He and a couple journalists were going around saying they were looking for missing guests. We don't know what that's about but I decided to take Interre out of the equation until we know more. The protest gave me cover to do it. Still deciding how to handle the two reporters.

"And one more thing you should be aware of: We haven't seen Faith Benedict since we got here. Not necessarily an issue—her staff's been cooperating with us and hasn't caused any obstruction—but it's a little unusual."

He exchanged a few more words and hung up. Just then a quiet beep indicated an incoming call. He picked it up and listened quietly, his face hardening.

"Fuck," he said after the caller had finished speaking. "What the fuck. Those assholes are gonna be so fucked when this is all over, but right now we just need to contain the situation." He nodded to himself. "Glad you found them and locked them up again. What about Interre?" Pause. "Shit. Okay. Keep looking for him."

He disconnected and let his eyes wander aimlessly over the revelers as his mind raced. He made a call and gave a short debrief, disconnecting with a frustrated sigh. He stood lost in thought again, checking his ring every minute or so even though it hadn't alerted him.

* * *

With what little energy it had after the escape, Bruno showed Louvin where Hiroe was. It expanded its awareness quickly toward and past the spot where they'd parted ways earlier and found her. Along with Demonte, they made their way to meet her.

Hiroe's eyes lit up when she saw Louvin, and Demonte tried for a neutral expression as Louvin scooped her up in a tight hug. "All right, lovebirds," Demonte said. "Let's hold off on the honeymoon a little longer." Hiroe extracted herself from the poet's arms with a sheepish smile. "Louvin's got a target on his back, so we're going to have to keep a really low profile from now on. Hiroe, did you find anything out?"

She related her encounter with Villanna to stunned faces. "I can't believe she lied to me," Louvin said angrily.

"I know," Hiroe said. "But at least she's helping us now." She pulled the other vial out. "She said this is safe to take even if you're not infected. I already took one and it's easy."

"Wait!" Demonte broke in. "You took some random shit some lady you just met gave you?"

Hiroe and Louvin both looked at him with irritation. "My sister is a brilliant nurse and scientist," Louvin huffed, apparently forgetting his own aggravation with her.

"It's easy for you to say that," Hiroe said to Demonte. "You weren't in the room with that—god, it was awful. I've never seen someone with aquamycosis in real life. I don't want to take any fucking chance of that happening to me."

"I wouldn't be taking shit that I'm not even sure the FDA knows about," Demonte said incredulously. "Plus she said herself it wasn't a cure, so even if it works, all it's going to do is hide the symptoms if you do have it. You won't even know for sure."

"It's just until we get through this," Hiroe said. "If I caught it, I don't want to start breaking out in fungus while we're down here trying to figure out what's happening. I'll get checked out later and see if I do have it. If I do, there's nothing that can be done than suppress the symptoms anyway, until they have a cure."

She turned to Louvin, hand outstretched, offering him the other vial. "Your sister said you should do the same."

Louvin took it, considered for a moment, then pocketed it. "I'll wait to see if I get any symptoms, and if I do I'll take it right away."

Hiroe looked like she wanted to object, but she bit her lip. "Okay, so what are we going to do about the missing lottery winners? That's the one thing we know nothing about so far."

"I think that FBI fucker—what's his name, Brooks?—took them," Louvin said bitterly. "He's an authoritarian pig."

"But why?" Hiroe asked. "And where are they if they're not in that building he's using as a jail? Could Bruno help us find them?"

Louvin shook his head. "It hasn't had enough contact with them to be able to home in on them, and besides, it has no strength right now. It needs to rest if it's going to be able to help us at all tonight."

Demonte broke in. "It'll be a total crap shoot wandering this fucking maze of a house trying to find them," he said. "And Louvin can't be out in the open where people can see him."

He sighed. "I'm thinking we'll have to hide you away somewhere and go back to the party. I'll see if anyone else saw the missing people leave or has seen them since, and Hiroe can find out what the scientists know about the disease jumping to humans."

Reluctantly Louvin agreed, and they headed toward the hallway of empty rooms where the breakout sessions had been held.

Hiroe turned the question of the missing people over and over in her head as they walked, looking for any halfway plausible theory. She scratched her cheek absently. Then the top of her head. Then her forearm, with increasing urgency, until it broke through her train of thought. She looked down and gave a horrified moan, stopping dead in her tracks. The other two stopped and they all stared at her arm.

A small patch of sickeningly bright green fungus bloomed there.

CHAPTER TWENTY-THREE

She touched the itchy spot on her cheek and felt an unfamiliar texture, feathery and rough at the same time.

She tore her eyes away from her arm and looked up. Demonte's and Louvin's expressions as they looked at her face confirmed her worst fear.

Wordlessly, Louvin withdrew the vial from his pocket and injected it into a vein on his forearm. "The fuck, man?" Demonte objected, his face a mask of despair. "Clearly that shit is not working on Hiroe. What good is it to take it now?"

Louvin shrugged tensely, his eyes filled with terror. "I've gotta at least try," he said.

Hiroe found her voice. "We've got to get back to your sister," she said. "She might have other ways to help us."

"Yeah," Demonte said reluctantly. "We can't go back to the party now. Even if this medicine was bullshit, she's our best—well, our only option. You know where she is?"

"She was going in the direction of the infirmary when I found her before, but she got a message and said she had to go. I don't know where to."

"We'll start with the infirmary," Demonte said decisively. "Let's get there fast, because I can't have *either* of you running into anyone now."

They reached the tunnel to the infirmary without encountering anyone and headed down it at a run. Hiroe was lightheaded but couldn't tell if it was a symptom or her terror. Her body felt unclean, unstable. She'd never experienced this sense of being invaded from within. She stumbled and caught herself, waving Demonte away when she saw him reach for her. "Don't touch me," she hissed.

They saw an attendant in a chair, seemingly guarding a door. Hiroe hung back, her face turned away, as Demonte and Louvin approached the young aquean man.

"I need to see Villanna," Louvin said. The man's eyes widened and he stood up in excitement.

"You're Louvin Interre," he said. "Holy shit! Aw man, I'm a big fan."

"Thanks, I appreciate it," Louvin said with as much politeness as he could muster. "Do you know if my sister's in there?"

The attendant disappeared into the room, the door sliding shut behind him before they could get a glimpse of its interior. Villanna emerged less than five minutes later, wearing a hazard suit with a full hood and transparent face piece.

Her eyes widened as Hiroe turned to face her, holding out her forearm. "My god," Villanna said. "I've never seen symptoms emerge so quickly after exposure, and to overpower the suppressant—I can't believe it!"

"Is there anything you can do?" Hiroe asked, outwardly calm.

Villanna nodded, thinking. "We have some other treatments in development … they're experimental, but your situation is so serious, we need to take some gambles." She turned to Louvin. "Have you had any symptoms?"

He shook his head. "I took the shot once I saw what was happening to Hiroe, so I don't know if I have it and it's being suppressed," he said.

"You both need to come with me," she said. "I'll consult with some of my colleagues and we'll figure out the best course of action. We can handle this, I think. But we need to start now. It's progressing very quickly in you, Hiroe. This is an aggressive form of aquamycosis and it's going to take aggressive treatment to combat it."

For once Louvin didn't argue with his sister. Villanna retrieved another vial of the medicine and gave it to Demonte. "You should take it too, now that you've been possibly exposed to it," she told him.

Demonte's face was inscrutable as he accepted the small object and pocketed it. "Think I'll wait and see if I get the symptoms," he said. "Thanks though. I appreciate having the option." Villanna pursed her lips disapprovingly but didn't press the issue with him.

Louvin unshouldered the bag containing Bruno and passed it to Demonte. "Can you take care of it for me?" he asked, sounding plaintive. Demonte hesitated, then relented, hoisting it onto his own shoulder.

"I'll go back to the party. You can find me there if you need me in the next couple hours," he said to Villanna. "Otherwise, I'll come check in with you when I leave it. Take care of them, okay?"

"I will," Villanna said earnestly. "Thank you for caring about my brother." Her voice caught, and she cleared her throat. Demonte nodded, his eyes turning worriedly to Hiroe, then walked away resolutely.

"Let's go," Villanna said to Hiroe and Louvin. They followed her into the infirmary. The door slid shut behind them and secured with a quiet beep.

Villanna led them through a nondescript white lobby into a room with several beds in a row and an array of equipment.

"Lie down and I'll get you comfortable while I go consult with my colleagues," she said. Louvin gasped, and the others saw with horror a small but distinct salmon-colored patch of fungus on the back of his hand. Before either of the women could say anything, a burly human attendant in a hazard suit entered the room.

"Should I get these ones processed?" he said to Villanna as if Hiroe and Louvin weren't there.

"No no," she said, her voice shaky but authoritative. "I'm taking care of these two. I just need them to … rest for a while."

The attendant nodded and went to a machine with a small penlike device hanging from it. He took the device and a retractable tube unspooled. He brought it to Louvin first. "This won't hurt," Villanna said. "It's just a medication to help you relax for a short time. Stress can trigger worsening symptoms, and I don't want you to suffer more before we have time to devise a course of treatment."

The attendant touched the pen to Louvin's arm and it emitted a short tone. He took a clear covering off the tip of it and put a new one on, then touched Hiroe's arm, just below the patch of fungus, which had spread an inch or two in every direction since she'd first detected it. She felt nothing when the device beeped. The attendant left without another word or glance in either of their directions.

"Get some rest," Villanna said tenderly, speaking to both of them but gazing at her brother. "I'll be back soon."

She too left, and the room became quiet. Hiroe and Louvin lay on their adjacent beds, staring at the white ceiling.

Hiroe's head swam as she relived the rapid escalation of events that had brought them here. She looked over at Louvin and nearly burst into tears when she saw a rusty reddish-orange spot marring the smooth green skin of his face, just under his right cheekbone. "I'm sorry," she tried to say, but her voice had deserted her. His face became blurry and the room began to spin.

Something occurred to her, and she spoke with effort. "What did that guy say—what did he mean by 'these ones'? Have there been others? You sister said it too—'these two.' What did she mean?" She began to feel nauseous, but then everything around her faded to nothing.

She realized her eyes were closed, and she struggled to open them. The lights in the room had dimmed, or maybe she was imagining it. She couldn't tell how long she'd been lying there; in some ways it felt as if she'd just blinked, but her body felt languorous, as if she'd been sleeping for hours.

She raised herself to a sitting position with considerable effort. Louvin was fast asleep on his bed, his visible skin now mottled all over with noxiously colorful patches she could see even in the dimly lit room with her blurred vision.

She looked down at her own hands and arms and saw that the fungus had spread even more on her. Her skin was now almost entirely covered, with just a few bare spots here and there. She felt horrified but in a detached, dreamlike way, as if she were in someone else's body observing what was happening to them.

Hiroe stood unsteadily, holding onto the edge of the bed for support until she felt able to stand on her own. She wasn't sure where she wanted to go; her body moved of its own volition despite her deep exhaustion. She stumbled toward the door and slapped at it clumsily until it slid open.

A corridor appeared in front of her, illuminated by strobe-like flickering lights. She wondered if she really was dreaming or if the drugs were affecting her vision. She followed the hallway, leaning against the wall every few steps to rest and regain her balance.

It stretched endless before her, until suddenly it ended at a door, which she pushed at until it opened into a large room. The light was glaringly bright, so much that a needle of pain stabbed her forehead. She squinted and blinked, waiting for her vision to adjust.

Suddenly everything came into focus, but her mind refused to believe what her eyes were seeing. She staggered back toward the door, an inarticulate wail escaping her lips.

CHAPTER TWENTY-FOUR

The room was flanked by two rows of rectangular trays, positioned just below eye level, each the size of a twin bed. Each held what appeared to be half-dissolved human remains, slowly melting into pools of liquid. Below each tray, a tube led to a large vat that seemed to be collecting the liquid from them.

Hiroe's glance skittered over the carnage, partial limbs, blood, innards, and bones in puddles of viscous ooze. Her eyes settled on a tray close to her. The face of the corpse was still partially intact, and she recognized the eyes, even in their lifeless staring state, and the wisps of colorful hair, remnants of an intricately twisted updo. It was Lottie.

* * *

Agent Brooks impatiently paced the party, dodging drunken guests. He checked in frequently with his team, frustrated by their lack of progress.

He stewed over Louvin's disappearance and the temporary escape by the protesters. He was considering making a visit to the prison to dress down the guards in person when someone entering the room caught his attention. A new course of action presented itself. He strode across the room.

"Hey, remember me?" he said cordially.

"Sure," the man said guardedly. "You're that fake security guy that hauled that aquean kid away."

Brooks chuckled. "You got my number all right. Name's Brooks. Agent Greg Brooks, FBI." He held his hand out, and the man shook it after a pause. "And you?"

"Demonte Sanders, Static News," he said.

Brooks nodded knowingly. "I could tell you were a reporter," he said. "You've been busy tonight, huh?"

"I guess," Demonte said in a noncommittal tone of voice.

"Look, I hope you're not sore about that kid," Brooks said in a reassuring tone of voice. "He's fine, I can assure you. We have every reason to believe he's involved in that protest, but we're not gonna do anything to him until we learn more."

Demonte shrugged. "I barely know that kid, just met him tonight," he said dismissively.

"But he was with you and that lady earlier, right?"

"Yeah," Demonte said. "They asked me to help them look around. I used to work with the lady, so I did her a favor."

"You said some guests had disappeared, huh?" Brooks said. "Well, after you told me that, I got curious. I started looking into it myself. And you're right—there's a few people missing. They're not in their quarters—they're not anywhere that my team's been able to look." He leaned confidingly toward Demonte. "There's something funny going on here, and I want to find out what it is. You know what else? I haven't seen Faith Benedict in person since I got here. Have you?"

"No," Demonte said. Something in his tone gave Brooks sensed he was holding something back.

"You know something about where she might be?" Brooks prompted.

After some hesitation, Demonte spoke. "The woman who was with me? She's a reporter too. She told me she was exploring the house, looking for the missing people, and ran across Faith Benedict's bedroom. Faith was in there and she was—well, my friend says she looked like she had aquamycosis."

Brooks didn't have to act shocked. He was caught completely off guard. "That's not possible."

"I know," Demonte said. "That's what I thought. But then my friend … it looks like she caught it from Faith. And she's human too."

He reached into his pocket. "She went to the infirmary to see if they could do anything for her. One of the doctors gave me this, told me to take it in case I'd caught it too." In his palm, a small clear vial with a rubber-tipped needle glistened.

Brooks stared at it, mind racing, digesting this new information. "But you didn't."

"Nah, man," said Demonte. "I'm not about to put some shit in my body when I don't even know what it is."

"I don't blame you," Brooks said. "And you haven't had any symptoms?"

"Nope," Demonte said. "Not yet anyway."

"Would you mind giving that to me? I'd like to look into this a little more."

Demonte hesitated, then shrugged and handed it over. "Sure, I don't plan on doing anything with it," he said. "If I were you, I'd get that over to the FDA or CDC. Seems like Faith's people are going a little rogue, and I don't trust it."

"Thanks, I'll do that," Brooks said, trying to hide his disbelief about how easy that had been. He pocketed the vial with caution, attempting to appear nonchalant about it. "Listen, I'm gonna keep trying to find out about those missing people. If you are too, we can help each other, share information."

"Sounds like a plan," Demonte said. "I'll keep poking around, I guess. It's probably nothing, but it's hard to keep that nagging voice quiet when you're a reporter." He smiled.

Brooks shook his hand again and the man left in the direction of the bar. The agent kept a casual, friendly smile on his face until Demonte had disappeared into the drunken throng. Then he lifted his ring to his lips and called headquarters.

He didn't bother with pleasantries. "The situation appears to have changed drastically," he said. "I may need to take the extreme measure." He explained briefly, then disconnected. He spotted a security staff member across the room and headed toward her.

CHAPTER TWENTY-FIVE

Demonte nursed a cognac as he made the rounds, talking to various guests. The mood of the room was joyful, almost bacchanalian.

No one seemed worried about the missing guests or concerned with the solemn reason behind the gathering; everyone was just enjoying the sumptuous refreshments and spectacular ocean views. The more sedate music of earlier in the evening had given way to upbeat electronic music and several clusters of partygoers around the room were laughing and dancing together.

People were more than happy to talk to Demonte, but keeping them focused was difficult, and when he did get them to answer his questions, they had no useful information. He felt at a loss as to where to go next. It was as if the missing guests had evaporated into thin air, along with anyone who knew them or had any connection to them.

He thought back over the exchange with the agent. He didn't think he'd given away too much, and he was more than happy to blow the whistle on the dubious medical practices happening in the mansion. Maybe Brooks was being sincere about sharing information, but even if not, hopefully learning about Faith's condition would turn his focus away from Louvin.

It couldn't hurt to at least pretend to be working together, so Brooks wouldn't suspect he'd had something to do with Louvin's escape. If there was security footage of him visiting the cell, Brooks must not have reviewed it yet—otherwise he'd have detained Demonte immediately. As long as the guards who'd seen him stayed at the prison, no one should have reason to connect Demonte to the breakout.

He abandoned the futile questioning of guests and stood in a corner of the room, watching the revelers from a distance and slowly sipping his drink. The problem was, once he wasn't doing anything that consumed all his attention, his thoughts turned to Hiroe. That didn't do him any good at all.

Not only could he not help her with the horrible problem she had now, but he'd vowed to keep his distance from her in general—and had managed to stick to that for the better part of a decade. Now that he'd spent several hours with her, he remembered why. She intoxicated him, made him feel like putty in her hands. He struggled against that and ended up acting like an asshole to her. It wasn't good for either of them.

She thought she was being subtle with Louvin, he was sure, but he could practically feel the chemistry between them. It had always been that way when they worked together, a parade of men in thrall to her. He hadn't witnessed it firsthand in years, having chosen to leave and co-found Static in part to escape her unintentional hold on him. He wasn't really surprised that in her fifties, she still had no trouble attracting men, and young handsome ones at that.

He tried not to resent her for it. She just didn't feel that way about him—he'd never sensed any opening to reveal his feelings—and so he'd set them aside as long as he could, and then gone on to pursue a new life when it got to be too much.

When she'd withdrawn completely from him after he told her he was leaving, he realized once and for all that he'd only been a professional convenience for her. Once he didn't represent opportunities for advancement anymore, Hiroe had dropped all pretense of being friends with him.

It was painful, but he was glad he'd found out and stopped clinging to the hope that beneath their camaraderie, she had deeper feelings for him similar to what he felt for her.

Now, seeing the beginnings of aquamycosis taking over her skin, it was even clearer that what he felt for her was much more than physical attraction. The thought of her being taken from the world was incomprehensible to him.

Something attracted his attention from the corner of his eye and took him out of his sad spiral of thoughts. He looked down. Louvin's satchel was emitting a strange light between the cracks.

He unfastened the top and opened it. Bruno's already garish yellow had become luminescent, glowing up at him. He looked around to make sure no one was watching. He wasn't sure what it meant, so he was about to close the bag when he saw that it was also pulsing ever so slightly.

"What the hell's wrong with you?" he muttered to it. He felt irritated having to take care of an entity he had no idea what to do with. He closed the bag and returned his gaze to the party.

He wasn't sure how much time had passed, but he suddenly noticed an entirely different sensation in his brain from anything he'd felt before. It was as if someone was inside him, trying to get his attention. He couldn't explain it to himself any other way.

He looked down at the bag again, and saw that part of Bruno was now protruding outside it. The glow had lessened, but he could see the shiny yellow clearly, touching his wrist. He jerked his hand away and immediately the strange feeling in his mind disappeared.

"Goddamn, Bruno," he said, still feeling foolish for calling it a name. "What the hell were you trying to do to me?"

As if in response, the luminescence increased and decreased in a slow flashing pattern. Demonte reluctantly realized that if he really wanted to know what Bruno wanted, there was an easy way to find out.

Gritting his teeth, he unfastened the bag and placed his hand gingerly on the mass. "All right, buddy," he said resignedly. "What've you got?"

CHAPTER TWENTY-SIX

He almost didn't finish the sentence, so overwhelming was the vertigo of connecting mentally with a nonhuman—but incredibly complex—entity. Bruno quickly and efficiently imparted its message to Demonte, not in words or pictures but in knowledge.

It was worried—or the slime equivalent of worried—about Louvin and Hiroe. It explained how aquean siblings share a psychic bond, so it was more attuned to Villanna than it was to most people. It was able to read nuances of situations if it was in the same room as people, and with people it was bonded with—such as

Louvin and, by extension, his sister—it was particularly sensitive.

And Villanna, Bruno sensed, was not being honest with any of them. It had been trying to tell Demonte since they'd left Louvin with her, but the slime's strength had been sapped by everything it had done tonight, and it had taken time to rebuild it.

Together, Demonte and Bruno relived the moments with Villanna. Demonte was able to see the interaction from Bruno's perspective, including the moments where it sensed deceit in Villanna's words or behavior.

Every ounce of skepticism he'd had about Bruno disappeared as he explored the being's complex awareness and understanding of things it witnessed. It kept zeroing in on a sense that Villanna's link with Louvin had weakened while she was talking to him, as if she was holding something back from him.

"You think we should go check on them?" Demonte murmured aloud. Bruno thought so. "Can you see if they're okay first, before we try and barge into a locked clinic?" It was as if

Bruno had been waiting for him to ask. Demonte's head swam as Bruno whisked his vision through walls and ocean—not even pretending to follow a route they could physically take—toward the clinic.

It homed in on Louvin and Hiroe. Bruno's vision was vastly different from human sight, so it was difficult for Demonte to make out what was happening, but they appeared to be lying on beds or examining tables side by side. The sickness had spread, Bruno sensed, and they were unconscious—sedated or resting naturally it wasn't sure.

They didn't seem to have attendants, not in the room at least. Bruno expanded its search slowly, discovering humans and aqueans as it went, at work or on the move in the infirmary.

"Can you find Villanna?" Demonte said.

It continued its expansion into the clinic, entering a room with many beds or tables, side by side. Demonte clutched his head with his free hand. Bruno was channeling an energy into him that felt very much like distress, and it overwhelmed Demonte, putting him in a panicked state.

He dropped his drink, barely hearing the glass shatter, and hurried toward the door at a near run. His hand was still half submerged in the mass in the partly open bag. Party guests looked at him with dazed, drunken confusion as he pushed through them.

He stumbled several times, bumping into walls, nearly tripping, his equilibrium shot. His vision doubled in a nauseating, disorienting way—he saw what was in front of him, but layered over that in his mind's eye, almost more vivid, was what Bruno was focused on.

It hadn't found Villanna. It had stopped when it encountered the cause of its current horror. The room it had expanded into housed as many humans as there were beds. But something was wrong. Most of them appeared to be dead, and their bodies were indistinct. Whole limbs or even torsos, sometimes heads, seemed to be missing or malformed.

Demonte couldn't tell if what Bruno was showing him was an actual representation of what was in the room, or an interpretation of the distress it felt. Either way, Demonte's nerves were overloaded with the intensity of Bruno's alarm.

Together they pounded through hallways and tunnels, Demonte panting and cursing the labyrinthine estate. At least there was no chance of getting lost; Demonte kept his hand on the yellow blob, and Bruno went off like an alarm in his head every time he even considered going in the wrong direction.

They reached the infirmary and Demonte stared at the door. "What now?" he asked, breathless from sprinting. "Should I try to knock?"

Bruno surfaced a suggestion. Demonte agreed with some reluctance. The slime around his hand thinned and molded itself to him. It didn't go transparent as it had on Louvin during the jail break, but it conformed itself to his hand like a glove. Demonte raised his hand toward the keypad on the wall. The majority of Bruno stayed in the bag; a rope of matter kept it from splitting in two.

Demonte watched, fascinated, as his yellow-coated hand seemed to move of its own volition, slowly tapping out a code. The door slid open. Bruno smoothly retreated from Demonte's hand and dropped back into the bag.

Demonte entered the room cautiously. It was bare and quiet. He opened another door, this one unlocked, and moved down the corridor it revealed, peering into door windows. He reached the end of the hall, one final door before him. There was no glass pane on this one. He touched it, and it slid open.

The moment it did, Hiroe, just on the other side of the door, practically fell into his arms. She struggled to get away, then realized it was him and collapsed with a sound of relief that was almost like a sob.

He stumbled back under her weight, and also in shock at her appearance. The fungus had spread to every part of her face and arms, a garish multicolored nightmare. If not for her familiar pageboy bob and the outfit she'd been wearing all night, he might not have recognized her at all. Her body felt as if she were wearing an uneven layer of padding under her clothes. But his dismay over her condition was soon overshadowed by what he saw beyond her.

"Lottie," Hiroe said, her voice odd and muffled. She gestured to the closest bed, and Demonte felt a shock of recognition at the partial face, the lifeless single eye staring at him.

"Holy fuck," he breathed. "What's going on here?"

CHAPTER TWENTY-SEVEN

Hiroe's mouth worked, but before she could attempt to answer, they heard voices in the corridor. "Hide," Hiroe said with effort.

Demonte looked around wildly, spotted a large cart full of unidentifiable devices on the far side of the room. He grabbed Hiroe's arm, wincing with worry at the feel of the fungus furring it, and pulled her with him.

They crouched behind the table. Hiroe attempted to still her breath. She tried swallowing but it was as if her mouth were stuffed with cotton. Her tongue felt thick and unwieldy, and its surface was numb. Her disorientation had receded, replaced by horror as she became fully aware of her disease-stricken body.

"The serum should be just about ready," a male voice said. "I'll check the levels; we may have enough by now."

A woman's voice replied, indistinct and muffled. The man seemed to understand what she said. "We'll have you undress and submerge in the liquid. These go in your nostrils to provide oxygen. It's very important for you to be completely immersed so we can treat your scalp and face."

Hiroe leaned against the table that provided their cover, wishing she could see what was happening.

Her eyes fell on Louvin's satchel.

She fumbled it open and laid her hand on Bruno. Demonte saw what she was doing and touched Bruno cautiously himself.

The connection was slower to come this time but built steadily, Hiroe thought. Perhaps the delay had to do with aquamycosis, or because Bruno was exhausted.

Then, just as Bruno's consciousness started to come into focus in her mind, Hiroe heard Demonte wonder if two people could communicate with Bruno at once. She looked in his eyes with a jolt, and they shared a silent moment of amazement. Somehow Bruno had given them access to one another's minds as well.

Sharing with a human mind was very different from how it felt between her and Bruno. Demonte's thoughts were almost like her own, instantly understandable, uncomfortably intimate and familiar. Staring at each other, knowing one another's thoughts, was disorienting.

Helplessly, filled with dread, Demonte saw his admiration for Hiroe laid bare before her, and felt her surprise and puzzlement as keenly as they both felt his own excruciating embarrassment.

He was too overcome to think about breaking the connection with Bruno. For several moments that felt like an eternity, he and Hiroe were locked in a ricocheting series of emotions. But they had no time to dwell on it; their attention was drawn to the scene that Bruno was revealing.

At first they saw it in Bruno's colorful, abstract way: a figure in a wheelchair, flanked by two others, one bent solicitously toward the seated one, the other adjusting controls on a large machine. But gradually, the combined efforts of their minds managed to translate and clarify what Bruno was showing them. It somehow started to resemble what human eyes would see.

The person in the chair came into sharper focus, and Demonte and Hiroe realized it wasn't just Bruno's vision creating the appearance of brilliant rainbow hues, but feathery rows of fungus, so thick it was difficult to comprehend someone was under it all.

The person's hair was nearly gone, the skull coated almost as thoroughly as the face and arms. A few locks remained, growing here and there between patches of fungus. Though it looked tangled and limp, the long silver hair still shone.

"I think we're ready, Mrs. Benedict," said the attendant near the large rectangular object.

The other attendant touched a button on the arm of the wheelchair and it rolled forward. Bruno turned its attention to them and the features came clear, visible through the clear plastic front of her hazard suit hood. Villanna Interre.

CHAPTER TWENTY-EIGHT

Hiroe was shocked. Then taken aback by how little this revelation surprised Bruno or Demonte.

Louvin's sister helped Faith to her feet. She unfastened her gown at the back and it floated to the ground. Demonte and Hiroe cringed at the sight of Faith's disfigured body.

Villanna operated a crane-like device, rotating its arm until it was next to where Faith stood, wobbling as if she were about to fall over. A flexible seat dangled from the arm of the device. Villanna helped Faith sit on it and secured her with straps.

Faith slouched tiredly as the crane lifted her up, then over the tank the male attendant had been fiddling with, and began to lower her slowly into it.

Her two attendants seemed transfixed by the process, so Demonte risked peering out from their hiding place for a clearer look than Bruno's vision could provide, his hand still pressed against the blob. Hiroe gasped as Demonte's view and Bruno's coalesced in her mind, giving her an almost more than lifelike vision of what was happening.

The tank was filled with a murky reddish liquid. Hiroe knew it was being fed from the trays where the bodies were being slowly dissolved. She wondered what happened to the liquefied remains as they passed through the machines before reaching the tank.

Faith didn't flinch when her head dipped below the surface. She looked something like an exotic fish, the frills of fungus swaying gently with the liquid until the ripples stilled. Her face, an expressionless multicolored mask, didn't move either. The bubbles emanating from her nostrils were the only indication she was alive.

Hiroe watched Villanna through Demonte's and Bruno's eyes with disbelief. The girl's face was suffused with excitement as she stared almost reverently at the tank. If she was bothered at all by Faith's appearance, or by the corpses around her, it didn't show.

Just then Villana blinked and looked around, wide-eyed. "What's wrong?" the other doctor asked.

"My brother," she said, frowning. "Something's changed with him. He's awake and worried." She took a last longing look at the tank, but there had been no noticeable change in Faith; she hung listlessly in the cloudy fluid. "I'll go check on him and the woman and give them more sedative if they need it."

Demonte ducked back behind the table, but Villanna didn't even turn in their direction. She hurried away, but Bruno was locked in to her now and the three of them followed her with their minds.

Before she could touch the door, however, it flew open and two people burst in. Villanna stumbled back.

Bruno's intuition told Hiroe and Demonte that one of the two was Louvin, though he was unrecognizable by now.

"Villanna!" he cried, speaking with effort, his voice sounding muffled. "Oh god. Don't touch me."

"What?" she said. "Oh. It's fine, my hazard suit protects me. But what are you doing out of bed, Louvin? You need to rest!"

He scrubbed a fungus-coated hand across his mask of a face. "Hiroe—she's gone," he said in a dazed tone. He pointed to the other person who had entered. "I woke up when he came in, and she was gone." He looked around. "Is she here? What's going on?"

"Jesus fucking Christ," said the person behind him in a choked voice. Bruno turned his focus to Agent Brooks as he surveyed the last of the human remains in the trays. "What the fuck is this?" Louvin took in the scene as well; Bruno could sense his rising horror and confusion. Brooks recovered and drew a weapon. "FBI—nobody fucking move!"

"Everyone calm down," Villanna said in a commanding voice. "Let me explain."

Just then, her colleague made a break for it, pushing her aside, stumbling over the wheelchair as he ran for the door. Brooks aimed his weapon and fired it at the man's chest. It made a quiet high-pitched tone and a flash of light and created a round, smoking hole in the doctor's hazard suit. He cried out and fell, feet from the door. Brooks pointed his lethal device at the man's head and discharged it again. His body jerked a few times before going still.

Bruno's reaction to the murder felt like it pierced Hiroe's and Demonte's temples. Brooks heard their cries of pain and turned toward the table. "All right, who's back there?" Brooks called. "Come out with your hands up."

Hiroe and Demonte reluctantly withdrew their hands from Bruno and emerged from their hiding place, arms raised.

"Stop," Brooks commanded, and they did as he said, hearts thumping with fear. Just then the agent's knees buckled and he fell to the floor, revealing Louvin behind him, wielding a long metal bar.

He raised it again, but Brooks was clearly knocked out. Louvin dropped his weapon and turned to Villanna, swaying slightly. "What is going on here, sis?" he said. The last word came out like *fiff* from his fungus-filled mouth.

"It's okay," she said soothingly. "You're going to be fine, and I can explain everything to you."

CHAPTER TWENTY-NINE

"Fine?" he said in a muffled groan. "Look at me. Look at her." He pointed at Hiroe. "We're going to die, Villanna."

"Of course you're not," she said. "You probably don't have aquamycosis, and even if you do, we've got the cure now. And Hiroe couldn't have caught it."

It was Hiroe's turn to break in incredulously. "But it can spread to humans now," she said with effort in a muffled, slurring voice, gesturing to the tank where Faith Benedict still hung limply from the sling. "And I do have it. It's all over me." She once again tried unsuccessfully to swallow, gagging at the thick numb feeling of her tongue and the inside of her mouth.

As she did, a few pieces of fungus became dislodged and fell out of her mouth. She coughed and more came loose. Parts of her tongue were now exposed. She tried scraping more out but it was difficult with her thickly coated hand.

Villanna raised her hands as if quelling a large unruly audience. "Have you experienced any of the symptoms that come along with the fungus? Weakening of the limbs, difficulty breathing, muscle pain? Of course not. What you have is a mild poisoning that mimics the visible symptoms," she said. "The fungus on you is annoying but harmless, and it won't last long. It'll fall off soon."

Hiroe felt a flash of hope but also suspicion and confusion. "What do you mean? How do you know?"

Villanna smiled tightly. "Because I gave it to both of you, silly. Or rather, you gave it to yourselves."

"I knew it!" Demonte burst out, and everyone turned to look at him. "Well, I did," he muttered. "It was those goddamn shots, wasn't it?"

Villanna nodded. "Yes, but it was to save both of them, I swear," she said.

"From what?" Demonte said sarcastically. "Seems like you were trying to put them *and* me out of commission to save yourself."

Villanna sighed. "Look," she said. "What we're doing is very important—life or death actually—for my people. We've isolated a certain genetic marker in some humans that, when their matter is applied topically to bodies afflicted with aquamycosis, causes it to retreat and die. We've never tried to wipe out a serious case until now—what we're doing tonight is historic—and we didn't want to try it on Faith until we'd tested it more.

"But when she began to deteriorate, we had to move quickly and we needed a lot of matter—more than could be taken from living humans; we needed several full bodies' worth. Most people's DNA is recorded in databases, so it didn't take long to identify humans with the gene we were looking for. We then chose people no one would miss. The lottery was a way to bring some of them here without arousing suspicion.

"Your meddling put our entire cause in danger. I could never kill my brother, even if he might ruin everything I've worked for" — she managed a glare at him — "but others on my team might, if they saw no other choice. I had to stop you to protect you."

"And you think that's fine?" Demonte said. "You're proud of working for people that would murder your brother and —" he gestured at the carnage around them " — do whatever the fuck this is?"

"To humans," Villanna spat. "Humans, who overran Earth and destroyed it, then damaged our oceans, then tried to annex what's left of them." She glared at them. "Did you know when humans first encountered aqueans, you captured us and put us on display on Earth? We were treated as freaks, even as we sickened and died, unable to acclimate to dry land or even communicate our pain. Humans have always treated us, the first people of Earth, the only true Earthlings, as second-class citizens."

"And isn't that how your people thought of your brother?" Demonte retorted. "You're cool with knowing they'd have killed him?"

"Sometimes a few smaller evils are necessary to achieve the greatest amount of good," Villanna said, with a slight hesitation. "Anyway, I protected my brother."

"Villanna!" Louvin cried. His voice still sounded muffled. He coughed, leaned forward, and spat out some of the fungus. It was less brightly colored than before and appeared to be withering. "How could you do this? Evil can't be countered with evil!"

Her lip curled. "And what *would* counter evil? Huh? Pretty words and speeches, paid for handsomely with humans' currency?" She scoffed angrily. "While you were putting on a show for the rich humans, I was back here doing the real work to help our people. The dirty work. The ugly work." She took the hood of her hazard suit off and threw it to the side defiantly. "*I'm* the revolutionary. Not you."

"What did you mean?" Hiroe broke in before Louvin could answer. All eyes turned toward her. She was shedding browning fungus faster than Louvin—patches of her skin were visible on her arms, face, and neck—and her speech was almost completely clear.

No one seemed to know what she meant, so she tried again. "Villanna, why did you say I couldn't get aquamycosis? I was exposed to it, possibly, just like Louvin."

Villanna hesitated. "Nothing," she said. "I made a mistake."

"How could you forget something like that?" Demonte asked. "You've been taking care of a human who's got it."

Just then they all heard a chilling noise, like someone thickly clearing a throat but inexpressibly alien-sounding. They turned toward it, toward the tank. Faith's ghastly face floated just above the liquid, staring at them through the glass.

"Nahh," she growled. She reached out for the side of the tank and began to hoist herself out of the fluid and over the side. They watched with sick fascination.

Though she moved slowly, it was a feat that would be beyond the ability of an elderly woman, let alone one who'd been bedridden, wheelchair-bound, and mostly catatonic the entire night. There was a strangely agile, strong quality to her movements. She was still coated head to toe in brilliant hues of fungus. Her remaining strands of silver hair were pasted against the growths on her head.

"What're you saying, Faith?" Louvin asked. He backed away slowly as she dropped heavily from the side of the tank onto the floor, crouching slightly as she hit. Murky fluid dripped slowly and thickly from the fungus and puddled on the floor around her.

She turned slowly. Her face was a mask, her eyes glittering from deep within it. Her mouth worked for a bit, grotesquely misshapen by the fungus that coated her lips, the inside of her mouth, and her tongue. "Nahh hwooman."

Villanna's voice broke the confused silence. "She's saying that she isn't fully human. She's part aquean. She's one of us, Louvin."

CHAPTER THIRTY

"Is that possible?" Hiroe breathed, her gaze momentarily torn from the mesmerizing spectacle of Faith's transformed body.

"It is," Villanna said. "It's very rare. Our species aren't very compatible in that way and don't often conceive when we have sex. And usually the children don't survive long even if they aren't miscarried. Those that do have a strong genetic tie to one parent or the other, so they look either aquean or human. As a result they end up being mistaken for—or passing for—the species they look like."

"But how—did that happen? And how has Faith kept it a secret?"

Villanna glanced at the figure. She looked down almost absently at her discarded helmet. "Faith told me what she'd heard whispers of growing up. That her parents had hired a young aquean man to be a nanny for her older brother and sister, and her mother became infatuated with him."

Faith had stopped moving. Her arms hung limp by her sides. The angle she held herself at seemed unnatural somehow. She stood, swaying softly, as if listening intently.

Villanna continued. "Her mother thought she was past child-bearing years, and she probably didn't even know there was a chance of conceiving with an aquean. There was even more ignorance then. Although Faith was born looking human, her mother's husband knew what she was, because he and his wife had not been intimate for years. Her birth father disappeared one day and was never heard from again, and her father decided to raise her as his own."

Louvin spit more dead fungus from his mouth, rubbed some from his arms. "When did you find all this out?"

"After I'd worked here a while," Villanna said. "When I first interviewed for the job, she asked me many questions about my family history. She said she was fascinated by our complex family structures.

"I later found out the reason she asked such in-depth questions was that she was always trying to find members of her real father's family tree. And she found one, in me." She smiled at Louvin. "In you, brother."

He was at a loss for words, so she went on. "Faith knew only a few things about her birth father: his first name and the general part of the ocean he was from. She eventually figured out his family name, traced his lineage, and discovered that I was blood related to her."

Tears sprang into Villanna's eyes as she looked tenderly at Faith. "She always felt drawn to the ocean, and when aquamycosis ravaged our people, she worked tirelessly to help find a cure, even before she was stricken herself.

"One day she revealed everything and told me about our connection. She asked me to keep it a secret so she could wield her human privilege to help our people more than she ever could if people knew." Villanna sighed. "I understood that she was right, so I agreed to keep it to myself, even though I longed to tell you, brother. I don't regret any of it. We've finally found the cure, you see? Look how strong she is—she hasn't stood by herself in weeks! She's getting better."

Demonte broke in. "She still looks completely fucked up to me. Plus, even if that's true, are you really saying we liquefy a dozen humans for every sick aquean?"

Villanna sent him a scathing glance. "Of course not," she said. "Faith's disease has progressed far more—she's lived with it far longer, thanks to our care—than anyone else has ever experienced, so we knew an intense dose was her only hope of recovering. We'll be able to give a smaller dose to people with less advanced forms of it, and once we discover what works about it, we'll be able to synthesize it. No more humans will need to die for the cure."

"What's she doing?" Louvin asked. His strangely calm voice caught all of their attention.

Villanna paused as everyone turned their eyes to Faith. She appeared to have grown several inches in all directions since she first emerged from the tank. She still stood in an unaccountably odd posture, and the riotously colorful fungus that covered her head to toe seemed to emit a faint glow.

"Faith?" Villanna said, with rising dread. "Auntie? You need to get back in the tank—it looks like you're about to spore!"

"Nahh aan-tie," Faith grated out through her furred mouth. "Nahh Fayh."

She stood straighter and walked toward them—if the bizarre set of movements that brought her closer to them could even be called walking. The group instinctively backed away as she approached. Villanna paused to pick up her helmet; her shaking fingers dropped it and she tried again.

The nahh-Fayh creature reached her and put its hands on her shoulders. Villanna looked up, her eyes like saucers. It leaned closer and suddenly breathed heavily into her partly opened mouth with a guttural hiss. Villanna screamed, shoved at it, and fell. She skittered away, half crawling, half sliding on the smooth clinic floor, clutching her hands to her mouth, and sat in a corner, shaking her head and moaning inarticulately.

The thing stood tall once again. The countless rows and frills of fungus swelled and moved. Demonte felt nausea rising but couldn't look away.

"She's going to spore!" shouted Louvin, stumbling toward the door of the lab. He grabbed his sister's arm but she pulled away.

"Didn't you see what just happened?" Villanna responded desperately. "The cure didn't work and she infected me. Stay away from me or you'll be dead too. Just get out!"

"Uh, guys?" Demonte gestured to Louvin's bag, which he'd dropped by his hiding place. The top had been forced partly open. Bruno was glowing an urgent yellow and spilling out of it.

Louvin made a movement as if to run over, then faltered. Faith, or whatever she'd become, stood between him and the rest of them.

"See what it wants!" he shouted to the man instead.

Demonte didn't hesitate this time. He ran over and laid his hand on the part of Bruno that bulged out of the opening.

Villanna was still sitting on the floor, staring at Faith. "I've never seen this much presporing activity on anyone!" she said. "This is going to be massive. Louvin, please, leave. Your friends will be fine, and I'm already gone."

Louvin paused longer, his eyes flicking over the scene. Hiroe had overheard enough of what Villanna had said. She ran over to him, sidestepping Faith, bits of dried fungus flaking off her as she did. "Come on," she said. She grabbed him by the arm and pulled him toward the door.

"Okay," Demonte said, looking down at Bruno. "You got it, buddy." Something about his resolute tone made the others stop and turn their attention to him.

He unfastened the bag and held the top open with both hands. Then he swung it back and heaved it forward, directly at Faith, who was about five feet away from him. He kept a grip on the bag, but Bruno slipped out and went flying through the air, a quivering, shifting yellow mass, landing squarely on Faith's fungus-crusted head.

CHAPTER THIRTY-ONE

The frills bristled all over her, as if sensing a foreign threat. Bruno was undeterred. It quickly thinned and spread until there was a yellowish, nearly transparent coating covering Faith head to toe. The others could still see the pulsing glow of her fungus through it. Bruno's own luminescence had faded as it stretched to paper thinness.

Everyone was frozen, transfixed. Faith's fungus swelled even more, as if trying to puncture Bruno like a balloon. But it remained whole, clinging to every inch of her.

The Faith-creature gave an inhuman screech of frustration. She flung her head back and the cry reached an earsplitting level.

Suddenly the fungus erupted from her skin, finally breaking Bruno's barrier, tearing him into shreds. Small bits of Bruno-covered fungus flew everywhere, spraying the room and splattering all the onlookers.

Hiroe saw Louvin wiping his face and chest. He'd been hit by a lot of it. Her heart sank. To have found out he probably didn't have aquamycosis, only to see him undoubtedly catch it in real time right before her eyes, was devastating.

But Louvin didn't seem to comprehend that, not at the moment. She realized he was trying to salvage pieces of Bruno, without success. The combined slime and fungus were fast turning into a viscous substance that oozed through his fingers and onto the floor. It was happening throughout the room. Louvin looked up at her with a panicked expression.

"You have to help me find Bruno, please!" he said. "It can't all be gone!"

She realized it was too late to try and extract Louvin from the situation unscathed, so she acquiesced. Demonte helped too, scouring the floor, equipment and anywhere the explosion had hit for any recognizable bits of Bruno. Villanna stood mournfully over the mangled, lifeless remains of Faith Benedict, whose body had been destroyed by the violent sporing.

"Everyone down on the ground!" A harsh voice rang out without warning, and they all jumped.

It was Agent Brooks. Conscious, standing, and holding his weapon.

Hiroe, who was closest to him, started to drop to her knees. Without warning, Brooks whirled and discharged his weapon.

Villanna fell clumsily to the ground, apparently in the midst of trying to rush the agent. She groaned in pain and clutched her shoulder.

"Villanna!" Louvin burst out. He involuntarily took a step toward her, and Brooks fired at him, putting a hole in his side.

The young aquean stumbled but didn't fall, and Brooks fired and hit him a second time, this time in his leg. He collapsed, but stubbornly crawled toward his sister.

Then Brooks put his weapon to the back of Villanna's head. "Wait!" Louvin cried. "Look at your hand!" Brooks paused, glanced down, and swore. Ugly green and orange patches of fungus bloomed on his skin.

"Don't shoot—she can help you," Louvin said. "Look, I'm already getting better." He rubbed more browning fungus from his face with the hand that wasn't clutching his side.

"I already took the cure you gave me," Brooks said. "I took it before I came here. It's fucking useless."

Demonte broke in. "That's just a symptom suppressant, and it was a faulty batch, as you can see. Villanna has a real cure, though. She gave it to them and it's working."

Brooks considered this, staring at the colorful patches growing on his hands. Hiroe saw her only chance. She charged shoulder-first into the agent, knocking him to the floor and landing on top of him.

He grabbed her arms and she could immediately tell she was outmatched. She clung desperately to him until he got a hand on her neck and started to squeeze. Hiroe fought to breathe, but his viselike grip tightened. Spots swam in front of her eyes and her hold on him started to weaken.

"Stop," a voice said. The agent's hands left Hiroe suddenly, and she looked up, gasping hoarsely, head spinning. Demonte had picked up the dropped weapon and put it to the man's temple.

"You got cuffs?" Demonte asked. Brooks nodded and reached toward his right pocket. "Stop," Demonte said again and the agent froze. Demonte nodded to Hiroe. "You get it."

She felt in his pocket and came out with a handheld device. As she turned it in her hands, trying to figure it out, Demonte had Brooks roll on his stomach and put his hands together behind his back. Hiroe touched one of his wrists with the device, hit a button, and thin plastic ties shot out and bound his hands.

Demonte knelt on him, a knee in the agent's back. "I got him—you wanna check on them?" he asked Hiroe.

She ran to Louvin first. He had a neat hole in his leg, another through his side. She didn't think either was lethal, but blue liquid was oozing from both wounds at an alarming rate.

Her sequined top was useless, so she tore off a strip of Louvin's own loose shirt and tied off his leg above the hole. She wasn't sure what to do with the wound on his side. She hurried to Villanna, also lying in a smear of blue blood.

"Tell me how to help him," she said.

Villanna opened her eyes with effort, and Hiroe pointed to Louvin. Villanna spoke with effort. "The cart … look for … cauterizer." She gestured weakly.

Hiroe ran to the table she'd been hiding behind mere minutes ago. She found the device, thankfully labeled, and took it back to Villanna, who gave her a few whispered instructions.

Hiroe returned to Louvin and gingerly tried it on his side wound in the front. His eyes flew open at the first sting of the device, but it worked, sealing his skin. He only flinched slightly when she repeated the procedure on the other side.

She was about to move on to the leg wound, but he put a hand on hers and she looked up into his eyes. "Help … Villanna."

Reluctantly she left him, hoping the makeshift tourniquet would be enough for the time being, and returned to his sister. "Where were you hit?" she said coldly.

Villanna turned her eyes to her. "Why bother?" she said bitterly. "The disease will take me and Louvin now anyway."

"We have to try," Hiroe said grimly. "Tell me how to fix you."

Villanna pointed to her right shoulder and unfastened the front of her hazard suit with her left hand. Hiroe pulled it off her right arm, pulled her shirt off her shoulder, and closed up the wound on both sides. Then she left her abruptly and returned to Louvin.

"Hiroe." Demonte's voice broke into her concentration as she closed the last hole in Louvin's skin.

Demonte still knelt on the agent, and he nudged the back of his head with the weapon. "Tell her what you told me," he said.

"You're dead unless you come with me," Brooks said.

CHAPTER THIRTY-TWO

Hiroe met Demonte's eyes. "What?"

Brooks continued in a monotone. "There's a bomb, and this whole place is gonna go in fifteen minutes. I triggered it right before I shot the girl."

"The whole—?"

"Everything," he said. "All the buildings. The main house, the prison, this place."

Hiroe struggled to comprehend. "But why?"

Brooks hesitated and Demonte prodded him again. "We don't have time for this,"

Brooks said, an edge of fear creeping into his voice.

"Then talk faster," Demonte said grimly.

Brooks sighed, but he had no choice. "I was sent here to assess Faith's progress in finding a cure for aquamycosis," he said. "We had advance knowledge of the plans for a protest, so we used that as our cover story to gain full access from her. The people I work for don't want a cure to be found."

"The FBI?" Hiroe asked confusedly.

"Not the FBI." He spoke rapidly, his voice inflectionless. "Aquamycosis was a lucky break for a group of—investors looking to annex more ocean territory. It's been very convenient in distracting aquean rights activists who have been trying to hold them back."

He nodded at Demonte. "When you gave me the cure—at least I thought that's what it was—I realized it was much farther advanced than anyone in my agency thought. I came here to verify it. It seemed like the cure was real, so I went to the final option—destroying it and all the research."

"What about all the people here?" Hiroe demanded.

Brooks continued flatly. "The tragedy will be yet another media distraction as well as getting rid of the cure—and all the people that helped find it, and many high-profile activists too. I was going to leave as soon as I set it. I'll take you all with me, but we've got to hurry."

Hiroe said, "So you're saying we can—?"

"Get away in water cars. Only I can tell you what direction we need to go to get far enough away so we don't die when it blows."

"How do you turn it off?" Hiroe demanded. "You set it with a remote control, right?"

He nodded. "But there's no off switch. Designed that way so no one could stop detonation."

Hiroe thought frantically. "There are so many people here!" she said. "Scientists, leaders, celebrities … did you say the activists? No, Louvin helped them escape."

"All recaptured," Brooks said levelly. "Now I suggest we get going."

Hiroe looked pleadingly at Demonte. "What should we do?"

He shook his head grimly. "I don't know, but if we just sit here, we're gonna die anyway. He prodded the agent again, more roughly this time. "Where's the bomb?" he asked him.

Brooks didn't answer, and Hiroe felt fury rising in her. "We're not going anywhere, so if you don't tell us where it is, you can just sit here and die with the rest of us," she said.

"Out there," Brooks said with reluctance, cocking his head. "In the sand, in that big patch of red coral."

Hiroe remembered the striking coral display from the VR tour. "That's not far from the trench," she said. "Would it help if we could get the bomb down there?"

"Don't know," Brooks said. "The only safe thing is to leave, but it's gotta be now—it'll take at least five minutes to get far enough away in a car."

Hiroe looked at Louvin and then Villanna. Both were weak and in pain. Trying to find the bomb would be out of the question for both of them. "Demonte, could you—do you think you could—"

He shook his head. "I can't leave you alone with him," he said. "If he hurt you, or got away and called his men—" He broke off, his eyes imploring. "Plus when it comes time to swim with the bomb—I'm just not that good. You are. It has to be you, Hiroe."

Icy dread gripped her, made her limbs heavy and weak. But there was no time to hesitate any longer.

CHAPTER THIRTY-THREE

She used Demonte's guest code to unlock a water car, then piloted it out toward the main house. She was already having trouble taking normal breaths, the interior of the vehicle bringing back memories of the one she'd nearly drowned in.

The lights throughout the garden still lit every feature brilliantly, and the red coral was easy to spot. She pulled the car to a stop in the sand next to it.

She fumbled in the back until she found the scuba masks and strapped one to her face with trembling hands. Then, fighting not to hyperventilate, she pressed the door open button.

The cold water washed in with a rush, the air inside the vehicle bursting from it in large clouds of bubbles. The pressure of the water pinned her against the interior for a few seconds, but once the vehicle was full, Hiroe was able to float toward the door and pull herself out.

Her limbs threatened to go catatonic as they had the last time she was in the water, but now there was no Louvin to help her. Louvin. She thought of the soft green of his skin, his expressive eyes, his trusting embraces. She thought of Demonte, of the ferocity of feeling she'd felt coming from him through Bruno. She felt strength returning to her arms and legs, and she swam.

At first she struggled to make progress, feeling hysteria rising in her chest, but then one of her hands caught the water just right, her legs bent and kicked out together, and she surged forward and was off. She ran her hands through the sand between pieces of coral, swimming over the bed, looking frantically for the bomb.

After what felt like an eternity, she saw a small green light flicker, dug her fingers into the sand, and unearthed the device.

It fit neatly in the palm of her hand. Hard to believe it could wipe out acres of buildings and hundreds of people in a flash.

She gripped it tightly, which hampered her strokes somewhat, and made for the trench.

The lights of the estate went right out to the edge, but the gap itself was dark and impenetrable. Hiroe steeled herself. Louvin. Demonte. She dove into the darkness.

She propelled herself downward, her legs finding their stride, sending her deeper as her hand skimmed the rock. The water seemed to grip her as she went down, feeling the side of the trench with her free hand, praying she could find her way back.

She lost track of time, intent on going as deep as she could as fast as she could. The weak green light of the device through her fingers was her only visible companion. Then she glanced at it again, and the light was suddenly red.

She didn't know if that meant there were five minutes left, or one, or thirty seconds. She drew her arm back and flung the device downward as best she could, hoping to give it some additional momentum as it sank.

Then she brought herself upright. She was now in full, complete blackness. She felt something soft and cool clutch her ankle and stifled a scream, imagining Elise's little hand, finally reuniting with her again. Kicking wildly, she shook whatever it really was from her leg. *I'm sorry*, she told her in her delirium.

She touched the side of the trench once more to orient herself, then flung her arms and legs into pushing her upward.

The motions and techniques had come back to her quickly, but her lack of practice in decades caught up to her now. Her shoulder and thigh muscles burned and her left leg twinged, threatening to cramp. She reached out and could no longer feel the wall. She couldn't see anything either. She closed her eyes and swam, expecting at any moment a blast that would end her consciousness for good.

Instead, she saw a growing brightness through her eyelids. She opened her eyes to the lights of the gardens. She'd drifted away from the edge of the trench during her blind upward climb, but it wasn't as bad as she feared. She struck out toward the glow, traversing the blackness of the trench below her, and swam past the red coral, past her incapacitated, waterlogged vehicle.

She hadn't had time to think about how she'd get back inside. She swam toward the main house, then tacked right toward where she hoped the infirmary was. Everything looked different from the outside.

Hiroe's mask vibrated suddenly, a short warning burst, and from the corner of her eye she saw a yellow light begin to flash. The filter was failing. Her chest tightened as if the air had already stopped flowing. Ahead she saw a building, she wasn't sure which one, and kicked faster.

A low booming sound came from behind her, accompanied by a tremor that felt like it went through her to her bones. Suddenly she was propelled forward by a forceful current of water. She was approaching the wall of the building fast, too fast. She reversed her stroke, trying to fight the water, but was unable to slow down.

She saw that the structure looming ahead of her was one of the tunnels connecting two buildings. Her mask vibrated again and the flashing light turned from yellow to red. In a last desperate push, she managed to dive lower, still pushed uncontrollably by the current. She felt her hair graze the underside of the tunnel as she passed under it. Her lungs burned as the mask lost power and the oxygen in the air she was breathing became depleted.

She plowed into the ground, sand and stones tearing into her skin as she skidded along the ocean floor. But it didn't matter because she was losing consciousness, her arms and legs helpless as her vision darkened.

The mask had become a suffocating prison and she tried to tear it off. But she didn't have time—the world went black and then it went away.

CHAPTER THIRTY-FOUR

The lights behind the bedroom curtain grew slowly brighter. They were programmed to mimic sunrise and sunset; when she'd first moved in, it had affected her mood not to have some sense of night and day. She was more acclimated now, but she still liked to start her day feeling like the sun was rising.

She was already beginning to stir, responding to the false daylight, when Louvin kissed her the rest of the way into wakefulness.

Hiroe rolled over and smiled at him. Sometimes she forgot momentarily when she awoke who would be next to her or if she'd be alone, but she could always tell before she opened her eyes. "What's up?" she asked sleepily.

"We have three graduates today, remember?" Louvin asked, stroking her hip and kissing her lips.

Hiroe sat up, all traces of sleep falling away. "I forgot!" she said. Her stomach fluttered with nervous excitement. She saw Louvin studying her face and knew he still worried about her, even though she'd taken this role willingly. She kissed his nose. "I can't wait!" she said.

Demonte came sleepily out of the bathroom as she approached it. She greeted him with a lingering kiss, still marveling over the strange twists of fate that had finally brought them together—and the fact that both her lovers had rescued her from the water on separate occasions.

After feeling the shockwaves of the explosion, Demonte had gone out looking for her and brought her unconscious body out of the water in time for her to be revived. Back on land, they'd danced around their attraction a short time longer, but it was useless to deny what they'd seen in one another's minds while connected via Bruno.

Demonte still ran Static but had moved in more or less full-time with her and Louvin. His news organization was a self-propelling juggernaut since breaking the twin stories of Faith Benedict's gruesome search for a cure and the attempts to thwart it. Brooks had been convinced to act as whistle-blower in exchange for Villanna's supposed cure for the aquamycosis he thought he had. By the time Brooks realized he didn't really have the disease, the story had broken wide open.

Hiroe reluctantly extricated herself from Demonte's embrace; she was already running late. She showered quickly and donned her wetsuit, then hurried downstairs barefoot to get a cup of coffee.

Since Villanna had inherited Faith's estate and vast fortune from prison, she'd shared it with Louvin so he could convert much of it into a healthcare facility treating aquamycosis patients, and the main floor was completely transformed.

Villanna and Louvin hadn't developed aquamycosis despite their extreme exposure to it. It didn't take long to discover that the combination of Faith's fungal invader's spores and Bruno had created a powerful antidote, and they'd gotten a megadose from the explosive sporing.

Luckily, Louvin had carried much of the substance away with him that night, thinking he might be able to find an intact piece of Bruno in it somewhere, and it had been studied and then synthesized.

The cure was widely available by now, but the estate was a coveted place for aqueans to receive treatment—though cases were dwindling rapidly, and there were fewer applicants every week.

On the main floor of the house, Hiroe stopped by a fish tank. She reached in gently and felt the stirrings of a presence in her mind. Louvin had eventually found a tiny scrap of Bruno at the bottom of his bag. Whether it had come off by accident when Bruno was flung at Faith, or whether Bruno had left a bit of itself deliberately, they weren't sure, and it couldn't communicate with them yet.

It was about the size of a tennis ball now, and its awareness was gradually growing in complexity every week. Louvin was confident most of its memory would come back in time, but it wasn't there yet. Nevertheless, Hiroe liked its gentle energy, its dawning curiosity.

She moved on to the cafeteria and poured a mug full of coffee, inhaling its aroma gratefully. The three bathrobe-clad graduates waved to her from a nearby table.

She brought her coffee over and gave them each a hug, then sat down and listened as they discussed their future plans now that they were completely clear of aquamycosis. Two of them—Extina, a young woman, and Bitt, a man in his fifties—were planning to return to live with family in their underwater villages, while the third, a college student named Davin, was going to make up his partly missed senior year on the surface.

They finished their coffee, and Hiroe stood. "Ready?"

She led them to a portal with a bottom hatch, where the graduates took off their robes, revealing sea-foam green skin, three unmarred bodies, free of any sign they'd had aquamycosis. Hiroe paused before she put on her mask. She'd performed her short speech many times before, but it felt new every time.

"I'm privileged to be your guide on this last leg of your journey back to health. Today will, in aquean tradition, link the three of you for the rest of your lives, no matter where you are or what else happens."

"And you!" Extina said with a smile, and the other two nodded eagerly. Hiroe's eyes welled up. She never asked for or expected it, but occasionally the graduates included her, and it hit her every time.

In the past, her cynical self-deprecating side would have told her it must be menopause causing all these emotions, but she found she had less use for cynicism these days. Instead she simply accepted the gift they'd given her with a smile, wiping away her tears.

She put on her mask, opened the hatch, and lowered herself into the water. She held onto a bar on the side of the portal until the others had joined her, then reached up and closed the hatch.

The motion-sensor lights of the garden came on as they approached, creating the sense that their path was being illuminated just for them.

The three aqueans swam joyfully in the open water; until patients tested completely free of disease, they could only use individual indoor pools where the water could be filtered and purified to avoid spreading infection. This was their first time in the ocean that they'd looked longingly at through the windows every day since their arrival.

Hiroe swam slightly behind them, happy to hang back and let them plunge toward it. She was just a ceremonial guide; graduates knew the way to the trench, had traced the path in their imagination many times before the day of the ceremony.

They passed the spot that used to be full of only red coral; its striking color had gradually been joined by green plants as the garden's artificial microclimates had been dismantled, but Hiroe would never forget the place where she'd found the bomb. Her chest tightened, but less than the last time she'd been out here.

After that it was a short swim to the edge of the trench. Here, if no one had invited her, Hiroe would wait at the edge while they completed the ritual, but today she would come with them.

The four swimmers paused at the edge, holding hands, looking at the opening, larger and more ragged from the bomb detonation, its darkness contrasting with the lights along the edge.

Hiroe squeezed the two hands she was holding. She met each graduate's eyes and nodded, then dropped their hands and took a deep breath. They dove into the darkness together.

ACKNOWLEDGMENTS

I couldn't do this alone. Undying gratitude to Jaclyn and Stevie, thoughtful and honest beta readers who have helped me improve several novels, including *The Infinity Cure*!